THE WELL-BEING JOURNAL

THE WELL-BEING JOURNAL

Drawing upon Your Inner Power to Heal Yourself

LUCIA CAPACCHIONE

NEWCASTLE PUBLISHING CO., INC.
NORTH HOLLYWOOD, CALIFORNIA
1989

ISBN 0–87877–141–7

Edited by Jim Strohecker and Nancy Shaw
Cover/Book Design by Riley K. Smith
Anatomical Drawings by Erik Andresen

The author of this book does not dispense medical advice nor prescribe the
use of any technique as a form of treatment for medical problems without
the advice of a physician, either directly or indirectly. The intent of the author
is only to offer information of a general nature to help you cooperate with
your doctor in your mutual quest for health. In the event you use any of the
information in this book for yourself, you are prescribing for yourself, which
is your constitutional right, but the author and publisher assume no responsibility for your actions.

A NEWCASTLE BOOK
First printing, February 1989
10 9 8 7 6 5 4 3
Printed in the United States of America

Dedicated
with
love and gratitude
to
my teachers:

BABA MUKTANANDA
Meditation Master
and
CHARLES EAMES
Designer/Filmmaker

and
TO ALL THOSE
PEOPLE IN MY SUPPORT SYSTEM
who have helped
in
my healing journey

THANKS

to the contributors:
Terry Chappel
Syd Field
Jill Jarrett
Maureen Moskin
John Stuart
Neil Tucker
Patricia Young

to all the students and clients
who helped field test the material in this book

to all the health professionals and teachers
who have instructed, inspired, and helped me
in my own healing and wellness

to my daughers:
Aleta Pearce
for word processing the manuscript
Celia Pearce
for her continued encouragement of my work

to my editors, Nancy Shaw and Jim Strohecker,
for their invaluable guidance and support

to the designer, Riley Smith,
for his enthusiasm
and beautiful presentation of my work

to the publisher, Al Saunders,
for his continuing support

Contents

Foreword

Ten years ago at Menningers, as I struggled through the treatment of a young female patient suffering from the terrors of a mental illness, I found by chance a book titled, *The Creative Journal: The Art of Finding Yourself*, by the then-unknown author with a long last name. It was Lucia Capacchione's first book on journal-keeping as a vehicle for self-discovery and healing. I bought the book and began to encourage the patient to keep her own personal journal as outlined. It helped her a great deal. Over the following years scores of other patients I have worked with have also used journal-keeping in conjunction with their psychotherapy, or other treatment as a way of assuming ownership for their lives and well-being. For me as a therapist the discovery of the book meant the use of another tool for treatment. For the patients it often meant a choice of continued illness or a journey into health.

Fascinating accounts of exploration and discovery have always held a special place in literature and art. Although the world's greatest explorers such as Marco Polo and Cortez have enriched history and made it memorable for us, there are other odysseys that are quieter and more private, yet provide invaluable riches for mankind. One such account is the basis of The Well-Being Journal. Lucia Capacchione writes in her storytelling style about her life and death struggle with a dread disease in which the collagen (connecting tissue of the body) degenerates. It was in the darkness of the crippling illness that she brought into play her own intuition and creativeness in reversing the process. In so doing she challenged the medical world by shedding new light on the healing power we all hold within ourselves. She brings to this story not only the realities of her own experience, but the clarity and definition of good science. It is a book about healing from within, an ancient idea with contemporary relevance. As the famous Spanish architect, Antonio Gaudi was so fond of stating: "Originality is a return to the origin."

The origin that Capacchione rediscovers is the healing power of integrating the mind, body, and spirit. Underlying all of her work is the simple but profound truth that each of us has within ourselves the power to change our lives in positive ways, including healing. Another theme throughout the book is the importance of attitudes and feelings as they relate to illness and health, and the importance of being in touch with this aspect of our lives. The old model of viewing the body as an organic machine that is fixed by mechanical or chemical manipulation is now being challenged by researchers worldwide. The Well-Being Journal is very timely as it is in the flow of knowledge that is confronting the limitations of both spirituality and science. What has often been seen as oppositional aspects of humanness have been very beautifully integrated in a process that is both theoretically sound and practical in application.

Following an account of her own illness and recovery, the book explores the issues and methods for creating or maintaining a sense of well-being. The author provides fascinating journal-keeping exercises, using the novel idea of writing with the non-dominant hand, a technique central to much of Capacchione's later work. By dialoguing with one's own body, a foundation of awareness and understanding can be established from which self-care and nurturing can develop. She then proceeds to guide the reader through a series of experiences designed to facilitate a process of healing. There is a simplicity and innocence in the way the book unfolds because it uses the tools and language of the child, yet it is profound in its impact.

While recently visiting the Menninger Clinic in Topeka, Ms. Capacchione was asked by a group of researchers if she would demonstrate her use of imagery and non-dominant hand writing. I joined the group to see what the experience would be like. She asked us to close our eyes and focus on various parts of our bodies. Then she had us draw a simple outline of the body. I began to cough at one point. We then colored in the areas of the drawing where we had experienced any tension, stress or pain. I colored the throat area red. In writing we then interviewed our distressed body part using our non-dominant hand to answer as the part. To my surprise, as I described my dusty and out of control throat and sinus, my left hand wrote, "I've had a cold and can't seem to get over it, and Granddaddy sold his stuff." To my amazement, the thought of my father-in-law's recent activities of moving into a nursing home, selling his home and household goods, and the sadness I felt about it came into my awareness. Within minutes my throat and sinuses dried up and the cough vanished. The method had been very effective in identifying the underlying issue of the persistent cough and allowed my body to take care of itself. The experience that afternoon was very useful not only in clearing up a persistent cough, but in confirming the validity and practicality of the ideas presented in The Well-Being Journal. It did indeed draw on my inner healing power which had not responded to a variety of medical interventions.

The experience also gave a richer meaning to one of my favorite quotes from Carl Jung. "Practical medicine is and has always been an art, and the same is true of practical analysis. True art is creation, and creation is beyond all theories. That is why I say to any beginner, 'Learn your theories as well as you can, but put them aside when you touch the miracle of the living soul. Not theories, but your own creative individuality alone must decide.' "

Robert E. Ault, MFA, ATR, HLM
Art Therapist
Menninger
Topeka, Kansas

CHAPTER ONE

A Journey of Healing

I don't believe that a person actually creates disease, but that his soul is expressing an important message to him through the disease.

—Arnold Mindell
Working with the Dreaming Body

At age 35, I came down with a life-threatening disease which turned out to be the greatest *teacher* I've ever had. This book is the result of the lessons I learned from that illness.

Although it seemed to appear suddenly, the illness had its roots in the dramatic life changes of the previous five years. It was a time when all my foundations of security crumbled. One after another, my old support systems collapsed. My parents separated after being married for thirty-five years. Since I'd always considered their marriage a rock of stability, I was terribly shaken up. Shortly after that, my own marriage of ten years ended abruptly, leaving me in a state of shock. This was followed by a bout with mononucleosis.

Within a two-year period, I moved four times and had a variety of free-lance design and consulting jobs. I was also adjusting to the challenge of being a single mother to two young daughters. With each major change, another rug was pulled out from under me: family, career, residence, health. Yet I struggled to remain "strong" for others, for my parents, and my two children. I was busy taking care of everyone else, but there was no one taking care of me.

After five years of trying to conduct "business as usual" in the midst of crisis, I collapsed. Under constant stress, my resistance fell and I became ill. The first symptom was extreme fatigue. Although it felt like mono-nucleosis, which I'd had two years earlier, it wasn't. The doctor at the medical clinic told me it was a "viral infection." Complete bed rest was prescribed, along with an antibiotic to prevent other infections. However, just the opposite occurred and I became worse instead of better.

I returned to the clinic many times that summer, saw a string of specialists, and battled the devastating side effects of medication. One episode included an error at the lab, a misdiagnosis, and the wrong pre-scription, leading to still further complications and infections. I spent many weeks in bed feeling like a victim of "modern medicine."

Day by day my illness and desperation increased. I was caught in a never-ending cycle of specialists, medication, and negative reactions to the drugs. The specialists could never agree about what my original illness was or what caused it. I had become afraid for my life. Many years later an iridologist told me I'd had a life-threatening disease in which the colla-gen (connective tissue) degenerates. I had literally come "unglued."

At this time my only relief came from writing and drawing in a journal, which I'd started keeping at the onset of the illness. My journal was the place where I gave voice to my feelings of frustration and fear. My fears became especially intense at night. Although I had never suffered from insomnia before, I was now chronically awake half the night. Often I got through it by writing and drawing in my journal:

> *My head has been aching, my body aching, my whole being hurting and confused—I want to free myself from this cycle which I seem to have been trapped in during the past months. . . .*

> *I feel like a ship without a rudder, no sails. Just floating aim-lessly. Trying to follow some current or other that will take me into motion . . . My emotions go up and down, up and down, like a rocking boat. It's tiring . . . Life used to taste so good—most of the time. I was enthusiastic and energetic. Now, that's gone and I feel drained, unsure, questioning the meaning in my life right now. . . . So I rest and sleep and read and think and*

reflect and review my life . . . and feel an important metamorphosis is going on in me right now and wonder how long the caterpillar will be in this cocoon and when and how the butterfly will emerge into the sunlight.

During this time I also had vivid dreams, and I got in the habit of writing, drawing, and reflecting upon them. One of the most powerful of these dreams was both prophetic and life-transforming. Here is the dream:

I am in a hospital on an operating or examining table. A woman Doctor is leaning over me from the right. She is embracing me—I am weeping quietly. She holds me and says softly, "Oh, you're afraid to die, aren't you?" And she holds me as if to say, "It's all right."

I awoke feeling incredibly comforted. The dream seemed so *real*, so tangible. In fact, it became a living reality not long afterward.

The woman in the dream entered my life a month later. Her name was Louise Hunt, a warm and nurturing woman who had a private practice in Creative Healing (a form of acupressure massage). She was recommended by a close friend, Sally, who had watched my condition go from bad to worse. My experience at the first treatment with Louise was identical to the one I'd had in my "healing" dream. When I left the session, I felt exactly the same as I had when I awoke from that dream: comforted. The beautiful atmosphere of her healing room and her serene attitude contrasted sharply with the cold, impersonal environment and treatment I had experienced at the clinic. My health started improving after only a couple of sessions with Louise, so I continued seeing her for several weeks.

After one of my visits, I wrote in my journal:

L. is healing me with her two hands and a bottle of oil—that's all it takes, she says, to do creative healing. But it takes more. It takes the kindness, compassion, caring, sensitivity, awareness, love that L. has.

How beautiful she is—her softness, her serenity and peace, her warmth, the tranquility of her environment at home. She exudes comfort—healing of mind-body-soul. . . .

She comforts me—makes me feel the way I did in the dream.

She helps me understand how my body works, what is happening inside, and she puts me in touch with my own healing powers, how my mind and emotions and body all work together.

L. is curing me—body-mind-soul—
with tenderness and touching,
touching tenderness.

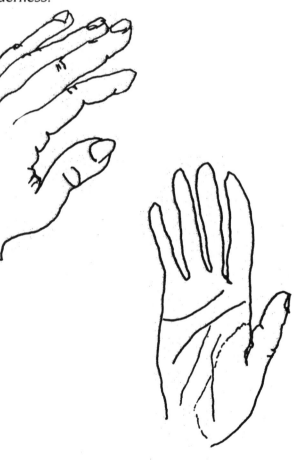

A PERSONAL SUPPORT SYSTEM

For the first time in my life I truly experienced being cared for in body, mind, and spirit. As my personal support system grew, I began to feel rays of hope. My gratitude to Sally for leading me to Louise Hunt was boundless. Phone calls and visits with Sally helped me out of the isolation of illness. On the days when I felt well enough, we did some professional work together, editing and illustrating a company newsletter. But what I remember most from the period of my illness is our long talks at my kitchen table, sharing our personal journals. We covered everything: our careers, our kids, our relationships with men, our experiences as women in the seventies. We struggled and laughed and cried together. Her intense blue eyes saw so much and she always told me what she was seeing.

Another key figure in my emerging support system was my mother, who took care of my two young daughters during the most difficult days of my illness. The circle of support widened when Carolina, an old friend and colleague, came back into my life. She suggested that I see a woman therapist, Bond Wright. I had never been in therapy before and was apprehensive, but something told me to make the appointment. My journal writing and drawing had shown me that body, mind, and emotions were all one, so it made sense that psychotherapy could help me heal from within.

When I entered therapy I never dreamed how powerful the transformation would be. Bond was a Radical Therapist who used an eclectic blend of Transactional Analysis, Gestalt Therapy, and Neo-Reichian body work. She was able to help me deal effectively with my rage toward the doctors at the clinic and excessive use of drugs. In Gestalt dialogues I yelled and screamed at them, even "beat them up" in effigy with a tennis racket. That was healing in itself and it really got my energy moving.

I developed such trust in Bond that I let her read my journals. She was highly enthusiastic and gave me great encouragement. Since I had dropped out of the medical clinic and had no physician, she recommended that I see Dr. Louise Light, who was in family practice. I liked Dr. Light instantly. An older, grandmotherly woman, she had been practicing preventive medicine for years, long before it became fashionable.

With great understanding and compassion, she helped me take charge of my own health. She really cared!

I stayed in therapy with Bond, who coached me to write weekly home-work assignments in the form of a contract with myself. She had me write these contracts with my awkward and unschooled non-dominant hand so I could access my Inner Child (feelings, vulnerability, playfulness, and creativity). In one session, I wrote:

> *Give myself*
> *permission to*
> *get well*
> *to move*
> *to feel my strength*
> *and aliveness*
> *and energy*

This process worked. I made a giant leap forward and my energy increased dramatically. Little did I know that the power of my "other hand" would play a significant role in my healing and complete recovery. Soon I found that while doing journal work, my left hand would spontaneously grab the pen and get its two cents in. My "other hand" wrote from a differ-ent "voice" within expressing feelings, intuition, and wisdom far more clearly than my dominant right hand.

In subsequent therapy sessions with Bond, we did Neo-Reichian work involving deep breathing while holding certain postures. This work releases powerful charges of emotional energy deeply held in the body in what Neo-Reichians refer to as "armoring." These energy releases were always accompanied by graphic imagery which appeared spontaneously in my mind's eye. These images revealed emotions I had been holding inside and mental beliefs that were causing inner conflict.

I recorded these images in my journal through pictures and words. They were incredibly helpful for they mirrored my state of being. I saw all the stress I'd been living with for so long. I saw and felt it releasing in my body. I *was* a quake-shattered earth. I *was* a high-tension wire that snapped. I *was* a bottle blowing its cork.

I walk a tight-rope – it moves
beneath me– I am afraid of falling–
it's so hard to stay up– so hard
so much tension in me– in the rope
– I am falling, falling

DEC. 10

therapy session with Bond

I have a block in my abdomen.
A cork. Heavy, hard.
It plugs me up. Won't let me out.
(Everytime I try to remove a cork from
a wine bottle, I mess it
up. The cork disintegrates
and I have to push
it down into the
bottle. And then I
push it in with
something.

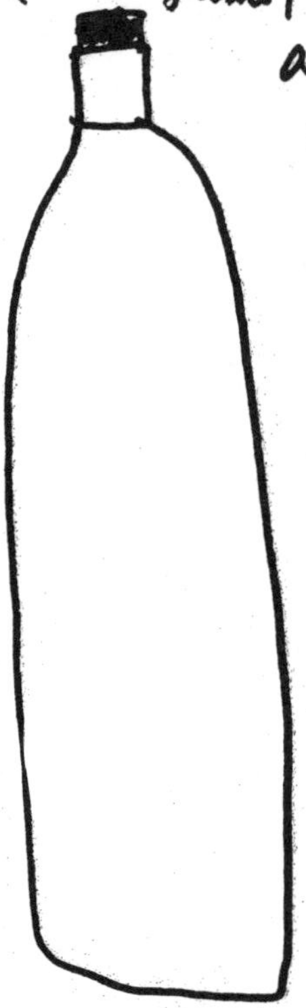

and the
wine
dribbles
out like
tears. But
doesn't flow
freely.

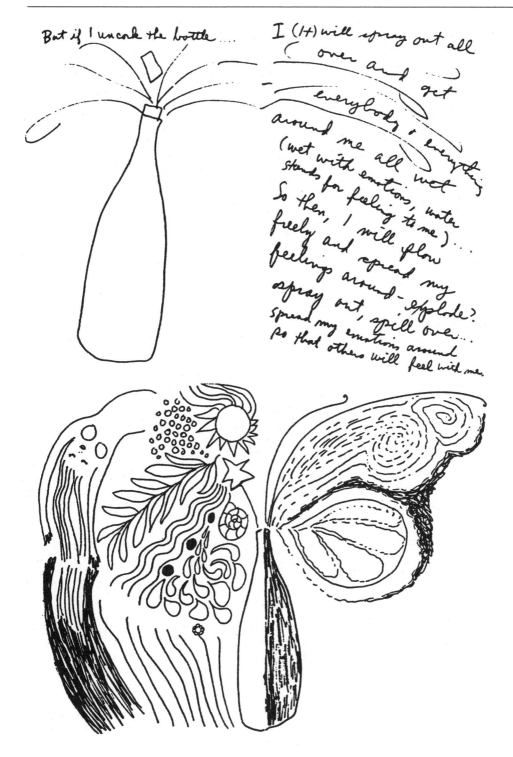

But if I uncork the bottle ...

I (It) will spray out all
(over and ...
— everybody, everything
around me all wet
(wet with emotion, water
stands for feeling to me)...
So then, I will flow
freely and spread my
feelings around — explode?
spray out, spill over...
spread my emotions around
so that others will feel with me.

THE PSYCHOLOGY OF THE BODY

As I reflected back upon my journal work, I noticed visual images and metaphors describing psychophysical states of being. I realized these images were nothing new. In fact, they have always been part of our everyday conversation: "She gives me a headache," "What a pain in the neck you are," "He blew his top." These images strike a chord in all of us. We understand them with our bodies, we "feel them in our bones."

I began to understand how physical conditions express feelings and beliefs which have been held in or denied. I recalled times in my own life when symptoms and pains disappeared as the stored-up feelings were released. I remembered throwing up right after being told some unpleasant news, demonstrating that "I could not stomach" what I was hearing. Then there were the ulcer symptoms which vanished overnight when a negative situation was brought to light and dealt with openly. And there were many confrontations I'd entered feeling weak-kneed, only to emerge with strength because I'd managed to "stand up for myself, on my own two feet, and hold my ground."

The more I delved into the realm of the unconscious through journal drawing and writing, the clearer it became that *the body is a physical expression of one's mental and emotional state.*

I began to understand why I had become ill. My body was speaking to me through my symptoms, saying: "Enough, Lucia. I can't take the stress anymore. I have to let go, sit back, relax." Like many of us, the only way I got rest was by being sick and going to bed. I had to have an *excuse* to sit still, get in touch with my Inner Self, and ask questions that had no quick answers, such as: "Where am I going?" "What do I want out of life?" I finally started to acknowledge and accept my exhaustion, confusion, turmoil. I stopped denying or fighting it off. When I started to *ex*press instead of *re*press, I felt better.

By drawing and writing in my journal, I learned that art imagery and written metaphors could yield jewels of wisdom buried inside my own body, inside my creative unconscious. Poetic and graphic images spoke eloquently of my state of being. The clarity of these images had healing power. When one of these images appeared it was as if a light went on inside my puzzled mind. I would respond, "Ah! So *that's* what's going on." This was always followed by a sigh of relief. Truly a breakthrough moment.

As I came back to life, the inner changes were reflected in my journal. The words and images began dancing across the page, transforming into poetry and drawings of rebirth.

TO DANCE. TO MOVE. TO SEE THE NEW CREATION FRESH. REBORN NEWBORN. SURPRISING GLISTENING AS DEW DROPS IN THE MORNING'S SUN - ON LEAVES OF LIVELY GREEN WET WITH EARLY LIFE. TO DISCOVER IN DELIGHT. TO BE. REBORN. I STRUGGLE FOR IT DAILY. KNOWING LIFE IS AHEAD AND I AM MEANT FOR IT. MAKING. LETTING MY INNER VOICES SPEAK. TO SING. A VOICE FROM THE DEEPEST. MOST QUIET OF MY SOLITUDES. TO SHARE MY ONLY-NESS IN CREATION. TO MOVE. TO LOVE MYSELF. TO WAIT UNTIL BIRTH COMES OUT OF ALL MY DYING PAST

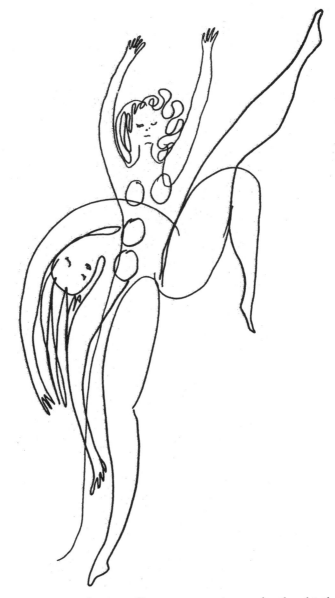

In retrospect I can see that my illness was an inner death-rebirth. The old, external structure of my life had fallen away and I had temporarily lost my sense of meaning and purpose. In becoming ill, I was forced into solitude and into myself. In confronting my fear of dying, I was thrown back into my inner resources, where I found truth. I was embraced by the recognition of a Higher Power within, and a whole new life opened up to me.

A NEW CAREER IS BORN

As the healing unfolded, I felt a dramatic increase in vitality and creative energy. After resuming work as an artist and teacher, it became clear that I had changed and my heart was no longer in my work. I wanted my professional work to reflect my new passion for personal growth, journal-keeping and creative healing. I found myself going through a career change.

Once again, I received encouragement from my support system. After seeing my journal drawings, my friend Sally exclaimed, "Lucia, you're doing Art Therapy here." I had no idea what she was talking about. I saw images of patients in mental hospitals doing basket-weaving. Sally explained that Art Therapy was a form of psychotherapy in which the client does spontaneous art followed by free association and interpretation with an art therapist. Her words hit home and I intuitively knew I had found my life's work. Through another friend, I was introduced to art therapist, Tobe Reisel. After six months of therapy with her, there was no doubt in my mind that this was the field for me. I entered a graduate program, received a Master's Degree in Psychology/Art Therapy and became professionally credentialed through the American Art Therapy Association.

As a Registered Art Therapist in private practice, I originated the Creative Journal method of self-therapy. I tested the method with my private clients and students in weekly classes. The results were astonishing. People reported major breakthroughs in their lives and frequently gave such feedback as: "This class was worth five years of therapy." I realized I'd found a direct and self-empowering tool for personal growth and change. My clients and students insisted that I collect my journal exercises into a book. They even offered to contribute examples from their own journals as illustrations. And so my first book was born—*The Creative Journal: The Art of Finding Yourself.*

Parallel with my professional work, my own studies led me deeper and deeper into the newly emerging field of holistic medicine. I had recovered from the disease, but now I was in search of optimal health. I read hundreds of books and personally experienced many different healing methods, such as Rolfing, Polarity Therapy, Chinese Medicine (acupuncture, acupressure, and herbs), chiropractic, sound and color healing, spiritual counseling, dance and movement therapy, hatha yoga, and meditation.

In my private practice, I began to observe that clients and students with physical problems were experiencing dramatic changes while working with my Creative Journal techniques. One of the most astonishing cases was a woman in her fifties who had suffered with chronic cystitis (bladder infections) for thirty years. Her physician had recommended exploratory surgery because she had had the condition for so long. She had been taking my Creative Journal class and decided to use one of my techniques —a written dialogue with her bladder—to see if she could get any relief. In her dialogue (which appears in my book, *The Creative Journal*) she uncovered a great deal of repressed anger and fear. The term "pissed off" immediately comes to mind as a common description of the connection between anger and the bladder. Shortly after doing this journal dialogue, the woman's symptoms disappeared and her condition cleared up entirely. When her husband became ill with terminal cancer awhile later, she dealt with it through journal writing. She also went on to teach Creative Journal to senior citizens dealing with aging, death of a spouse, and other life changes.

Another student, a young woman named Pamela, healed a chronic physical condition by getting in touch with its psychological roots. While taking my first Well-Being Journal class, she wrote a dialogue with her sinuses, which had been congested since early childhood. Pamela used my technique of writing with both hands. She wrote her own voice with her dominant hand and let her sinuses speak with her non-dominant hand. Regressing to early childhood, she experienced the time when her parents divorced and left her to live with her grandparents. She had been a "brave little girl" and held back her tears. While printing, "I really want my mommy," with her nondominant hand, she cried and released years of grief and sadness. Her sinus problems gradually disappeared. Pamela's profound experience inspired me to begin writing *The Well-Being Journal,* and I started gathering my class notes into a handbook.

In 1979, I was invited to teach at the Center for Healing Arts in West Los Angeles. Founded by a psychologist, Dr. Hal Stone, the Center pioneered counseling and self-help support groups for cancer patients and their families. The Center provided me with the perfect opportunity to field-test and refine *The Well-Being Journal* method. In working with seriously ill patients who were dealing with life-and-death issues, writing with the "other hand" was the one technique that consistently resulted in personal breakthroughs. My research there led to another book, *The Power of Your Other Hand,* which is devoted solely to that technique and its many applications.

Continuing my research, I went on to develop a private training program for health-care professionals: nurses, physicians, body workers, and therapists. Many of these individuals went on to integrate *The Well-Being Journal* into their work with patients and clients. The journal process has proven especially valuable for hospitalized patients and for individuals dealing with life-threatening illnesses.

As the field of holistic medicine developed in the late 1970s and early 1980s, more programs and support groups like the Center for the Healing Arts were established: the Center for Attitudinal Healing in Tiburon, California, the Wellness Community in Santa Monica, the L.A. Center for Living in West Hollywood, Louise Hay's Hayride, to name a few. I have had the privilege of leading workshops at the L.A. Center for Living for AIDS patients and others with life-threatening or chronic illnesses. The atmosphere of safety, support, and caring in these groups is both comforting and deeply empowering. I have also learned a great deal about how essential a support system is in dealing with crisis through my seminars for cancer patients at the Wellness Community.

It has been gratifying to see the beginnings of scientific research that validates my experiences with healing. Most notable is the work of psychologist James Pennebaker at Southern Methodist University in Dallas, Texas. Pennebaker's research showed that writing and talking about an illness experience actually strengthened the immune system and led to fewer doctor visits. In recent years there has been a great deal of research on the functions of the right and left hemispheres of the brain. It has been discovered that visual imaging (a right-brain function) can play a role in healing minor as well as major diseases, such as cancer and leukemia. I look forward to psychological research which further explains the healing power of the non-dominant hand and its connection to the right brain.

I am greatly encouraged by the progress in holistic health care since 1973, when I lived through my own death-and-rebirth experience. In looking back I see that all the basic ingredients of my own healing are at the heart of the holistic movement: *self-reflection* (in my case the journal process); *body/mind work* through therapy and physical nurturing; a personal *support system*; and spiritual tools for coming home to *one's Higher Power or Inner Self.* The most important message I learned from my disease is that the healing process is activated by a spiritual force that resides within us. It has always been there and is only waiting to be called forth.

THE JOURNAL PROCESS

A journal or diary is an excellent tool for developing awareness and powers of self-reflection. Each time you make an entry into your journal, you open another door into yourself. It is not surprising that throughout history artists, scientists, philosophers, and explorers have used journals or diaries to record their feelings, thoughts, observations, and discoveries. Inspired by this tradition, *The Well-Being Journal* encourages the inner exploration so characteristic of psychologists' and philosophers' journals. It also fosters the sensory observation that typifies the notebooks of scientists, explorers, writers, and artists.

Journal-keeping is one of the best ways to gain insight into oneself. At the same time it is a wonderful tool for developing creative abilities and communication skills. The privacy and personal nature of the journal make it a perfect vehicle for spontaneous expression and discovery. Journal-keeping that is done for yourself alone provides one ingredient so essential to true exploration: freedom from externally imposed standards and judgments. The journal is a safe place to be yourself: to feel, to think, to observe, to dream. As long as it is kept confidential, except for selective sharing, then the threat of external criticism is removed. The only critic you are left with is yourself (and often we discover that we are our own worst critic).

This brings me to one of the most common obstacles to journal-keeping: self-criticsm. But then, self-criticism is probably the biggest obstacle to trying *anything new.* Regarding drawing and writing in the journal, the most common objections are: "I can't draw," "My writing is terrible." "I don't have any talent," "I'm just not creative." All I can say is that you need no specific talent or training in the arts to do the exercises in this book. This is not a course in the arts or creative writing. You are *not* being asked to produce Art or Literature, to please anyone, to get grades or approval, or to meet outside standards. You *are* being encouraged to relax and allow yourself to explore writing and drawing as a means for greater awareness and self-knowledge.

You may find that you enjoy writing and drawing once you've had the chance to do them in a safe, nonjudgmental atmosphere. Most of the illustrations in this book were done by students and art therapy clients who began with the same feelings of inadequacy about drawing and creative writing that most people have. In fact, even those who have had training and experience in drawing and creative writing (including myself) have approached this type of journal work with some uneasiness. For in therapeutic arts the emphasis is on art-for-personal-growth's-sake. This is quite different from the approach found in schools and museums, so the trained artist or writer has no particular advantage here. Remember, the therapeutic arts are not about performance or the end product. The goal of arts and writing therapy is the *self-understanding of the person creating the art.* There are no right or wrong results. There is no external goal or standard of judgement. There is only personal expression, self-observation, and (hopefully) insight.

The illustrations in this book are meant to show you how others have responded to the exercises. They are not meant to be copied or imitated in any way. Follow your own impulses and intuitions; develop your own style and approach.

USES OF ART AND REFLECTIVE WRITING

One of the most exciting developments in psychotherapy in the past two decades has been the emergence of Art Therapy. Many noted physicians on the leading edge of body/mind healing have incorporated Art Therapy techniques into their work. Bernard Siegel, M.D., (*Love, Medicine, and Miracles*) and Martin Rossman, M.D., (*Healing Yourself*) direct patients to draw their illnesses on paper. Many exercises in this book are based on Art Therapy. For instance, the following is a basic Art Therapy technique:

1. The client or patient makes spontaneous art by drawing or painting feelings, a life situation, or a dream.

2. The client/patient then talks to the art therapist about the images, symbols, colors in the artwork. This is often done in free-association, using the art expression as a reflection of the unconscious. It is like having a dream in tangible form and then deciphering the hidden messages.

In Art Therapy, the verbal response of the client or patient is usually spoken. In *The Well-Being Journal,* the response is *written by* the journal-keeper *for* the journal-keeper. It can also be used as an adjunct to therapy, to be shared with the therapist when appropriate.

While I'm on the subject of therapy, let me share a word of caution: *This book is NOT a substitute for professional help if you need it.* Rather, it is a tool for maintaining better mental and physical health. In using these exercises you are applying principles of preventive medicine and holistic health. You are sharpening your sensory awareness and paying close attention to your whole being: body-mind-spirit.

If you are ill or convalescing from an illness, writing and drawing could have immense value for you. Journal-keeping is an ideal medium for anyone sitting in bed all day with nothing to do. Such expression can enrich the healing process. Instead of seeing illness as an enemy who attacks from outside and must be gotten rid of as soon as possible, you might learn to view illness as a gift from the Inner Self, an opportunity to put your whole being back into balance.

Illness can be a great teacher from within. A journal can be a "living text-book" for learning the lessons that the illness has to teach. If it had not been for my own illness, I would not have gone in search of well-being, nor found the vitality and enthusiasm for life I enjoy today. I would never have shared journal-keeping with the thousands of people I have now reached through books, workshops, and private counseling.

WRITING WITH YOUR OTHER HAND

As you do the exercises in this book, you will find instructions to write with your non-dominant hand. It will probably feel awkward, slow, and the writing may appear barely legible. You may find yourself wondering what the benefits could possibly be. Let me explain my research and experience.

It is an established fact that the right side of the brain controls the entire left side of the body. Furthermore, in recent years a great deal of research has shown that each hemisphere seems to specialize in certain functions. The left brain contains centers which control speech and logical, analytical thinking. The right brain specializes in visual/spatial perception, emotional expression, and intuitive abilities. Our society has emphasized left-brain logic and goal-orientation, and has thereby restricted development of right-brain skills.

My research shows that no matter which hand you normally write with, your non-dominant hand accesses abilities associated with the right brain. The non-dominant hand writes from a different voice within. It expresses feelings, intuitions, and wisdom far more clearly than your dominant hand. It uses simpler words, more poetic images, and reveals more profound insights. In writing with your non-dominant hand, you will be tapping into the creative and healing power of your right brain and directly applying it to your health and well-being. (For a more in-depth treatment of this subject see my book, *The Power of Your Other Hand.*)

GUIDELINES TO JOURNAL-KEEPING

The Well-Being Journal is like any tool. It works only if you use it. The benefits you receive depend upon the following:

1. Your willingness and active involvement in journal-keeping.

2. Your desire to honestly explore and express yourself to yourself.

3. Your commitment to living a healthy and fulfilling life.

The exercises are arranged in sequence and grouped according to themes. I suggest you *do the exercises in the order given.* This will help you build a solid foundation of skills in awareness, self-reflection, and personal expression. The instructions are divided into sub-sections. *Read each sub-section and do it,* then go on to the next sub-section, continuing until you've completed the exercise.

Once you have done the exercises in sequence and familiarized yourself thoroughly with the material, use the book in any way you wish. Think of it as a reference guide like a dictionary. Follow your own needs at any given time. Find the technique that feels right for you by using the Table of Contents, in which the exercises are listed by name and thematic grouping. Improvise and expand upon the exercises. Invent your own. This is not a textbook to be followed unquestioningly. Rather, it is a guide into your self. The better you get to know yourself, the more unique and creative the personal expression in your journal is likely to be. Enjoy being and expressing YOU.

TIME AND PLACE

Use the journal whenever you want, when you have something to explore or express. It is not necessary to work in your journal every day, but the more you use it the more you will benefit. If you want to use it daily, set aside a special time each day such as bedtime. You might also want to carry your journal while traveling or whenever you go out if you think there will be an occasion to use it. It's a great companion when you have extra time on your hands. If you're recording dreams, it's important to have the journal at your bedside. That way you can draw or write the dreams down upon awakening. You can always go back to them later for interpretations and insights.

Keep your journal in chronological order. Date the first page of each day's entry. This will enable you to go back and review your life as it happened.

Find an environment that is conducive to meditation, relaxation, and self-reflection. The physical setting is an important aspect of journal work. It is most helpful to have a quiet and private space. Choose a comfortable place where you are free from interruptions and distractions.

Reserve a period of fifteen minutes or more, depending upon how many exercises you wish to do in one journal session. Some exercises take longer than others, so plan accordingly. Don't rush. Journal-keeping yields the best results when you're totally focused and involved, not hurrying to get it over with. Don't make it into dutiful "homework." Embrace it as a gesture of self-love and nurturance.

HONESTY AND PRIVACY

An essential ingredient in journal-keeping for personal growth is honesty. For this reason it is important that your journal be kept private and confidential. If you are worrying about the reactions of others, it will be difficult for you to be honest and spontaneous. You might start editing or rethinking what you REALLY feel in case someone looks at your journal entry. Remember, one of the greatest values of journal-keeping is that it is a form of inner communication and self-therapy. *Protect your right to privacy and keep your journal in a safe place.* Do not leave it around for others to pick up and browse through. If you share space with other people, establish ground rules or arrange some means of protecting the privacy of your journal.

SHARING

Journal work does not flourish in a hostile atmosphere. If you want to share your work with someone, find a loved one, a trustworthy friend, or a counselor who understands you. It is especially nice to share with another journal-keeper. Someone who is also involved with the process will be more likely to offer understanding and encouragement. Avoid those who are judgmental and critical of you. When I first began keeping a journal during my illness, I shared it with my therapist and a very close friend who also kept a journal. I received lots of affirmation from both of them for what I was doing, and the sharing helped me out of a sense of isolation and loneliness I'd experienced while ill.

MATERIALS FOR JOURNAL-KEEPING

1. A *notebook*

   - Unruled white paper
   - Convenient size (6" x 9" or 8 1/2" x 11")
   - Durably bound so pages don't tear or fall out easily and can be kept in chronological order

   I recommend one of the following notebooks:

   a. A blank book (hardbound or paperback) with unlined white pages. Available in art supply, stationery, or book stores.

   b. A spiral-bound sketch pad with unlined paper. In art supply, stationery, or dime stores.

   c. A three-ring loose-leaf folder with plain white, unruled paper. If you prefer typing the verbal material, this is the best book for you.

2. *Writing and Drawing Tools*

   A set of fine-point colored felt pens or pencils in eight or more assorted colors. This is the minimum for writing and drawing. If you wish to try other drawing media, here are some suggestions:

   - Medium or wide-tip felt pens
   - Crayons
   - Oil or chalk pastels (with spray fixative to prevent smearing)

PREPARING TO WORK IN THE JOURNAL

When you are ready to work in your journal, reserve a period of uninterrupted time—fifteen minutes or more. If you want to begin with the Breathing Meditation and Inner Journey, it is best to add an extra ten minutes to your journal work period.

Be sure that the place you've chosen is comfortable and free from distractions. Journal time is *your* time to be alone in blessed solitude. Don't let anyone or anything encroach upon this very special time with yourself. For some, taking "alone time" may be difficult to do at first. Look at it this way: taking time out *just for yourself* is the first step toward better health. You deserve it!

Date the first page of each day's entry before you start working. No matter which exercise(s) you choose to do in any given journal session, it's a good idea to begin with the Breathing Meditation or your own favorite relaxation technique. Relaxation is restful and healing. It regenerates the body and mind and opens up awareness, intuition, and creativity.

Now you are ready to begin. Enjoy the journey into yourself.

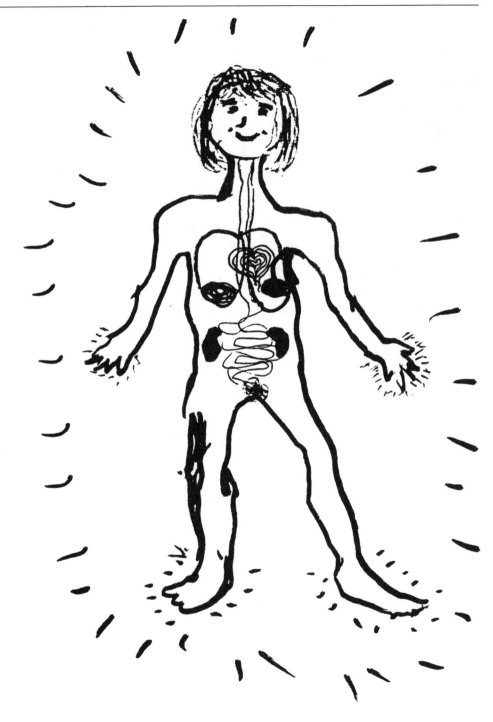

CHAPTER TWO

Body Awareness

PREPARING TO DO JOURNAL WORK

Your body is talking all the time. It speaks to *you* through inner sensations; it speaks to *others* through facial expressions and body language. It is constantly sending cues about your physical, emotional, mental, and spiritual states of being. The question is: Do you *listen* to your body? Do you *tune in* to the subtle as well as obvious messages your body sends you? Do you *take time* to hear what your body needs?

Most of us listen to our bodies with only half an ear. We pick up *strong* signals about the need for food, drink, temperature changes, exercise, rest, sleep, and elimination, and we usually respond. But sometimes we misinterpret or even ignore these and subtler cues. This happens especially when we are under stress. If we do this repeatedly, we run the risk of becoming ill. For instance, Janet gets signals of emotional upset through a "nervous stomach." Instead of identifying the disturbing emotions, she tries to get rid of the physical symptoms. She eats and drinks although her body isn't really hungry or thirsty. She gains weight and also develops chronic stomach discomfort. She then gets medication to deaden the pain (temporarily), but it doesn't go away. The cause of the upset has not been addressed, only the symptom has been treated. It's like cutting weeds. If the roots aren't pulled up, they grow back over and over again.

Another example is Larry, an ambitious businessman who suffers from fatigue. He chooses to work long hours night after night, seven days a week, even though his body wants sleep and his brain needs a vacation. When was the last time *you* succumbed to external pressures or self-expectations that ran counter to your emotional/physical needs?

This chapter contains techniques for listening to your body. You'll learn simple ways to quiet down, relax, and pay attention to your body. Then you'll express the body messages on paper through drawings and written dialogues with body parts. You'll learn to create change through pictures. Knowledge of textbook anatomy is not required. Your body will teach you what you need to know. It is your living, breathing guide to greater vitality and better health. Listen to the wisdom of your body.

BREATHING MEDITATION

This is an exercise in breathing to be done in a quiet, private place. No distractions, no interruptions. Allow this very special time just for yourself.

In order to relax and breathe fully it is important that your spine be straight. So I'm going to give you some simple directions for a reclining posture that will help you relax.

Lie on your back on a carpeted floor or firm bed. Your legs are straight and slightly separated. Feet are twelve to eighteen inches apart. Your arms are at your sides about a foot away from your body. The palms of your hands are facing upward. Your chin is tipped slightly down toward the chest to elongate the neck. The back of your head is resting comfortably on the floor or bed.

Close your eyes and relax your body and mind. Focus your attention on your breathing. As you inhale and exhale, listen to the sound of your breath.

Notice *how* you are breathing. Are you breathing through your nose or your mouth? Be aware of the rhythm of your breathing. Is it fast or slow? Observe *where* you take the breath into your body. Do you breathe sigh into your upper chest or lower down into your abdomen? How *much* air do you take in? Is your breathing shallow or deep?

Now relax and breathe through your nose. Inhale and exhale in a smooth and effortless rhythm. As you inhale, feel the air nourish and refresh your entire body. As you exhale, let the breath carry away tension and worry.

Gradually allow your breathing to become deeper and slower. Don't force the breathing. Just allow the air to come in and go out in a steady flow. Slowly let your chest and abdomen expand, as you fill up with air. Then release the breath naturally, letting go more and more. Relax into your body and the natural rhythm of your breathing. Feel how relaxed you are.

Benefits: This exercise will help you slow down and become more aware of one of your major life supports—breathing. It will also help you learn to relax and tune in to your body sensations.

INNER JOURNEY

Now you will take a long, leisurely inner journey through your body. Close your eyes and take this trip slowly. Remain lying down comfortably on your back as you practiced in the breathing exercise. As you go on your inner journey pay attention to everything you feel inside.

Imagine that your consciousness is shrinking down to a tiny point at the top of your head. You might see it as a tiny flashlight or a miniature hand. You are going to travel inside and feel the sensations in each area of your body.

Start at your forehead. Feel the sensations in this area. Do you experience tension or do you feel relaxed? Observe how your forehead feels. Then *slowly* move down your face. Check out the sensations around and behind your eyes. First your left eye and then your right. Do you feel strain or fatigue there? Or are you relaxed? Then move to your nose, cheeks, and sinus area. Observe the sensations there. Are you breathing openly ? Or are you congested? Now slowly move down to your mouth, your chin and jaw. How does this area feel? Is it tense or relaxed? Go inside your mouth and check out the sensations in your tongue, gums, teeth, and other areas there. How does it feel?

Now move up to your ears. Check the sensations in and around your ears; first your left ear and then your right. Then go around the back of your head and gradually move up to the crown. Be aware of any feelings there. then travel around inside your brain; first the left side and then the right. How do these parts feel? Observe all the sensations there.

Next, travel slowly down through your head to the inside of your throat. How does it feel there? Is your throat open or is it constricted? Does it feel good or is it sore? Check out your neck, both the front and the back. Is it tense or relaxed? Observe all the sensations there. Next, observe the feelings in your shoulders and the joints which connect your arms to your body. Be aware of the left shoulder joint and then the right. How do they feel?

Travel slowly down your arms; one arm and then the other. First, observe the feeling in your left arm. Start with the upper arm, then move down to the elbow. How do these areas feel? Then notice the sensations in your left forearm and wrist. Be aware of your left hand. Check out the palm, the back, and then each finger of your hand. How do they feel? Then repeat the journey, this time traveling down your right arm. Again, start with the upper arm, moving down to the elbow. Notice all the sensations as your awareness moves from one area to the other. Observe the feelings in your right forearm and wrist. Then notice the sensations in your right hand: the palm, the back, and each finger.

Return to your torso. Move slowly down the front. Observe the feelings in your chest, heart, and lungs. Is this area tight and held in? Is it open and expansive? Do you inhale easily and deeply and exhale as naturally? Or do you experience constriction and difficulty in breathing fully? Travel next to your digestive system and through your stomach. How does it feel there? Move down to your bladder and internal organs. Move down to your intestinal area. If you feel sensations inside but are not sure which organ is causing them, simply note the sensations and the location. What kinds of feelings are you picking up in these areas? Next, move down to your genitals. Experience any sensations you are feeling in this area of your body.

Now, return to the back of your neck and observe the feelings in your upper back and shoulders. Is there tension and soreness there? Or do you feel loose and relaxed? Move slowly down your spine, down the middle of your back. Then observe feelings in your lower back and pelvic area. Is there any stiffness or soreness? Do you feel comfortable and relaxed? Continue down to the base of your spine, your anus, and buttocks. What kinds of sensations do you experience there?

Finally, move down your legs. Begin with the left pelvic joint and travel down your left leg. Observe the sensations in your left thigh. Then move down to your left knee. Are these areas tense or relaxed? Move gradually down the calf. Then check out all the sensations in your ankle. Lastly, move down into your left foot: the top, the sole, and then each toe. How does the foot feel? Now, repeating this journey, move your awareness gradually down your right leg. Start with the right pelvic joint and check out the sensations in your right thigh. Then move down to the knee. How does this area feel? Then move down your right calf to the ankle. Then check out your right foot: the top, the sole, and then each toe. What sensations do you feel there?

Relax fully and do a quick review of this inner journey. Make a mental note of any areas of stress, pain, or discomfort.

When you inhale, consciously send the breath to those areas of your body. Take plenty of time. In this way you are nourishing the parts of your body that need tender loving care.

Benefits: This exercise is intended to help you stop, look, and listen to your bodily sensations, and to become more aware of what is going on inside you. When used regularly, this meditation serves as an important feedback tool, an early warning system for catching symptoms of stress before they develop into full-blown illness. In conjunction with the next exercise, it can also help to get to the roots of chronic ailments. You can become fluent in the language your body speaks: nonverbal feelings and sensations. In this way you will become more sensitive to your whole self, opening up communications between your mental/ emotional nature and the physical aspect of your being.

You will be using the Breathing Meditation and Inner Journey repeatedly throughout the course of this book. Many have found it extremely helpful to have an audio tape of the narration. For this purpose, I have created the *Well-Being Journal Meditations* audio cassette tape. The meditations are accompanied by original music and include other journal activities found in this book. To order this cassette contact: INNER-WORKS, 1341 Ocean Avenue #100, Santa Monica, CA 90401. If you prefer to record the exercises in your own voice, you have my permission. Of course, reproduction for commercial use is prohibited.

BODY MAPPING I
Charting Sensations in the Body

Do the *Breathing Meditation* and *Inner Journey*. Then ask yourself:

How do I feel right now?

Review the sensations you felt as you did the meditations. Locate the areas where you felt strong sensations: tensions, pain, soreness, irritation, pleasure, relaxation. Let yourself really feel the physical sensations in your body.

Choose the appropriate body map on the following pages. *(Photocopy the body maps so that you can have extra copies whenever you do the exercises that involve mapping.)* Color in the areas where you feel sensations with colors, textures, shapes, and lines that express those sensations.

After coloring in the body map, write down your reaction to what you have drawn. What is your body map saying about your physical condition at this time? What about your emotional state? Is there any connection? What about your mental state? Do you see any connection between that and your physical sensations?

Benefits: Through mental and graphic picturing, body mapping helps you experience and locate sensations in your body with precision and sensitivity. This is a good way to learn more about anatomy *from the inside.* If you want more technical information on anatomy, see Bibliography.

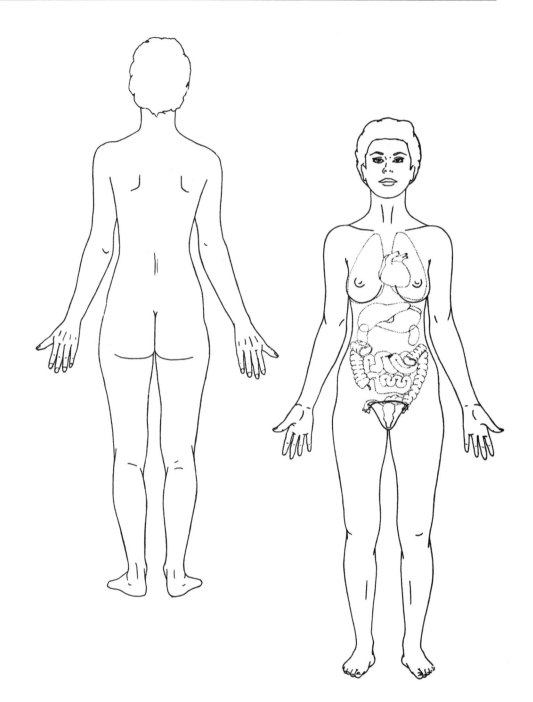

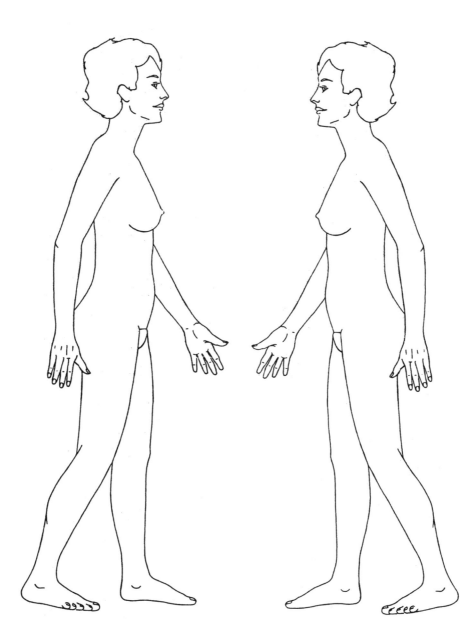

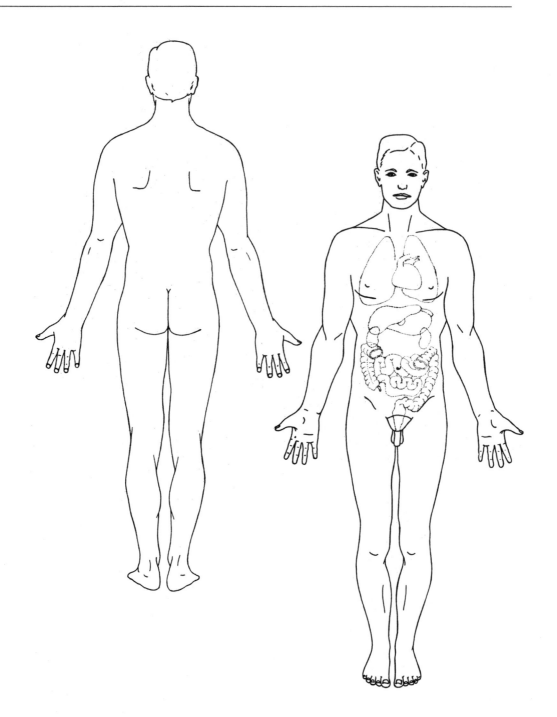

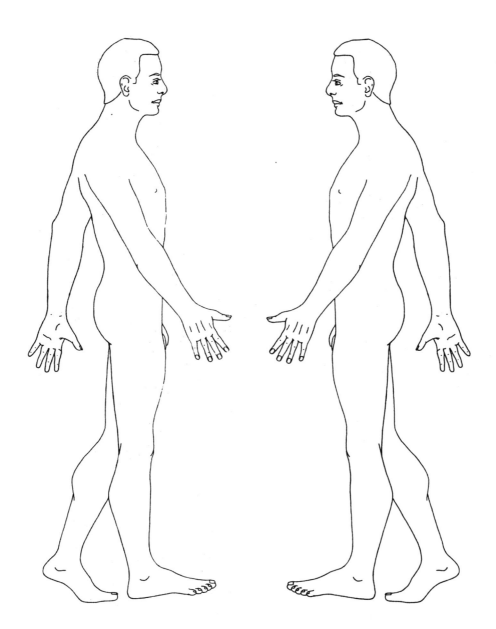

BODY MAPPING II
Drawing How I Feel

Do the *Breathing Meditation* and *Inner Journey.* Then ask yourself:

How do I feel right now?

Close your eyes and experience the feelings inside your body.

Draw a freehand picture of your body which expresses how you feel. If you are nervous about drawing, remember it can be very simple (a cartoon, stick figure, or silhouette). You're *not* expected to make art for exhibition. Rather, you *are* getting in touch with your body and expressing its messages through drawing. Let your drawing reflect the physical sensations in your body. If emotions and feelings come up, include them also. Write the names of sensations and feelings in or around the drawing.

Benefits: Here is a tool for further developing your ability to visualize. It is a means for using drawing in the service of awareness and well-being, a way to sensitize you and help you communicate with your body. This exercise helps you verbalize through labeling physical sensations and emotions.

THE BODY PARTS SPEAK

Do the *Inner Journey*. Choose the body part in which you felt the strongest sensations and draw a picture of it.

Interview the body part using the questions listed below. Write the questions with your dominant hand, let the body part answer with your non-dominant hand. Use a different color pen in each hand. Don't preplan the dialogue. Let it happen spontaneously. Don't worry about spelling, grammar, syntax, or vocabulary in writing with the non-dominant hand. It often speaks and writes a language of its own, disregarding rules and conventions. Although your non-dominant handwriting may be awkward, slow, and barely legible at first, as you continue the initial frustration and difficulties will lessen. Remember, this is a great opportunity to experience a breakthrough in old patterns and access intuitive wisdom.

1. Who are you? or What are you?

2. How do you feel?

3. What caused you to feel this way?

4. What do you want me to do for you? How can I help you?

In your dialogue, the non-dominant hand may have given you guidance on how to help you feel better. Draw a picture of your body reflecting any healing that has taken place. Now, with your non-dominant hand, let your body describe how it presently feels.

Benefits: This is a method used in Voice Dialogue and other forms of role-playing. It helps you get out of your head (rational, left brain) and into your creative unconscious (intuitive, right brain). It helps you express the wisdom in your body, letting you go directly to the inner source for some of the answers to your questions.

DIALOGUE WITH BODY

Right Hand: Who are you? Identify yourself.

Left Hand: *I am your body.*

Right Hand: How do you feel?

Left Hand: *Good, but there's a dull throb in my stomach and a tight-ness in my right knee.*

Right Hand: Which is giving you more pain right now?

Left Hand: *My right knee.*

Right Hand: What caused you to feel that way?

Left Hand: *Stiffness and accident.*

Right Hand: What was the accident that caused your right knee to hurt?

Left Hand: *Hitting on the sprinkler playing lawn football. I wanted to damage myself.*

Right Hand: Why did you want to damage yourself?

Left Hand: *Because I didn't belong.*

Right Hand: Who or what did you want to belong to?

Left Hand: *My family. My mother was dying and I wanted to punish her.*

Right Hand: Why did you want to do that?

Left Hand: *Because she left me alone.*

Right Hand: When did she do that?

Left Hand: *When I was a baby.*

Right Hand: What can I do to heal you? to make you feel better?

Left Hand: *Let me alone—love me.*

Right Hand: Which is it?

Left Hand: *I don't want her to die. I will be alone. Nobody loves me.*

Right Hand: I love you.

Left Hand: *You hate me. You force me to do things when you want me to, not when I want to.*

Right Hand: Are you angry?

Left Hand: *Yes, you don't listen to me and then you yell at me and say I'LL SHOW YOU.*

Right Hand: What can I do to correct that—to heal that?

Left Hand: *Accept me as I am.*

Right Hand: Are we still talking about the right knee?

Left Hand: *No—about my stomach and rectum. I want to hold on. If you don't love me I'LL SHOW YOU.*

Right Hand: What would you like me to do to accept me as I am?

Left Hand: *Be patient and don't leave me alone.*

Right Hand: Like mother did?

Left Hand: *Yes.*

Right Hand: You're not alone and my mother's dead.

Left Hand: *No she's not—she still forces me to do what I don't want to do.*

Right Hand: What don't you want to do?

Left Hand: *Go to the bathroom when I don't have to and wet my bed.*

Right Hand: You don't have to do that anymore. I can help you. What can I do to help you let go of those old thoughts and feelings?

Left Hand: *Let me go!*

Right Hand: How can I do that?

Left Hand: *Release me.*

Right Hand: Tell me how to do that so I can help you.

Left Hand: *Trust me, love me, listen to me.*

Right Hand: I need your help. Guide me so I can trust you and love you and listen to you. What can I do to do this?

Left Hand: *Go inside and find your True Self. I will show you every-thing, I will show you the way.*

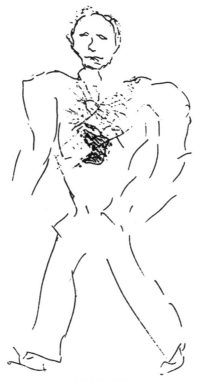

HEALING
(Written with Non-dominant Hand)

My stomach is healed & feels soft and warm like a ray of sunshine on the face. I glow like the morning sun and am loose & feeling good. It feels so good to be free of pain & filled with LOVE. I am love and like the sun I reach to darkest corners & bring them light. I am the truth, the light.

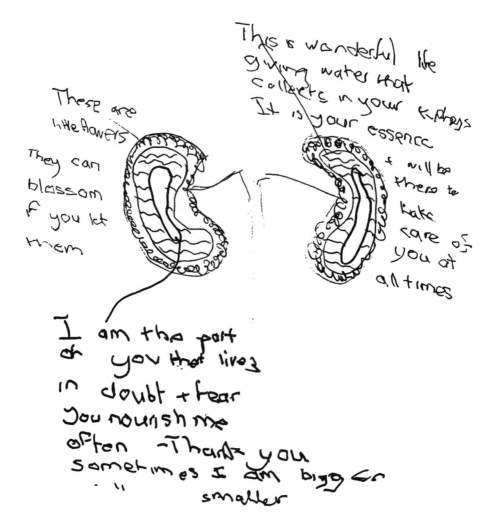

These are
little flowers

They can
blossom
if you let
them

This is wonderful life
giving water that
collects in your kidneys
It is your essence
& will be
there to
take
care of
you at
all times

I am the part
of you that lives
in doubt + fear
You nourish me
often —Thank you
sometimes I am bigger
smaller

DIALOGUE WITH KIDNEYS

Right Hand: Who are you?

Left Hand: *I am your kidneys. I am in your lower back.*

Right Hand: How do you feel now?

Left Hand: *I feel like I want to swim away to a very happy, relaxed &
joyful place & not have any problems.*

Right Hand: Why do you feel that way?

Left Hand: *I am tired of coping with all your stupid damn problems— you never let me do the work I need to do to heal you and help you so go & take a jump. I hate you. You're a bully. You don't trust me.*

Right Hand: What can I do to help you?

Left Hand: *You must start running on the beach again. I enjoy that. I can feed you my precious water & get fed from the ocean. Did you know we are connected. I love being there.*

We could be really good friends you know because I really admire you at times. You have much courage & energy. But you never let my voice get through. Sometimes I long for you to admire me & listen to the important things I have to tell you. We could be a GREAT team. I have so much wisdom. Don't you know I am your other half—not your better half just your other half.

Please stop worrying. You waste your wonderful energy. It's misdirected. When you think you have a problem send it over to me. I'm the one that's meant to deal with problems.

Right Hand: What else can I do to help us work together? I'm tired of feeling run down.

Left Hand: *Can you believe that it's really easy to feel better. Just ask me. Let me feed you from our wonderful resource. I like the herbs. The vitamins are so-so. The best thing for us is to stop worrying and thinking you have problems. All we have are challenges & always the means to meet every one of them if we just learn to work together.*

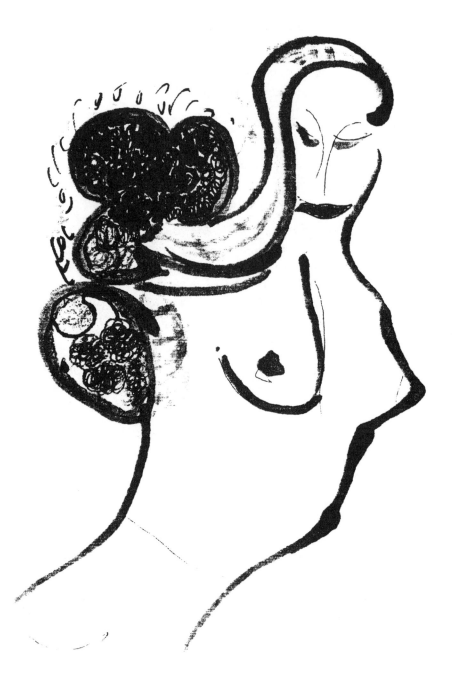

CHAPTER THREE

Body Image: History and Beliefs

Your attitudes and beliefs about your body create an image which lives inside you. This image or mental picture has a powerful impact on your body. *You are what you believe.* Your body image influences how you feel, how you move, as well as how you affect others. You also have *the power to change what you believe* and thereby change your body.

For example, one of my students—a woman in her mid-thirties—had grown up being constantly told by her perfectionistic parents that she was awkward and clumsy. She came to believe this was true. In order to avoid further humiliation, she stayed away from sports, dancing, or any physical activity in which she might be subjected to ridicule or criticism. These experiences deprived her of the very activities which would have developed motor coordination and self-confidence. In my class she confronted her belief system by using some of the exercises in this chapter. While in the process of reshaping her beliefs she also took a dance class with a supportive teacher whose approach helped reverse the damage done by her parents. She discovered a newfound grace and fluidity of movement that she never thought possible.

In this chapter, you will explore your body image. You will identify what you like and don't like about your body and where you acquired these attitudes and judgments. You will also learn how to turn negative beliefs into positive ones. In this way you can embrace ALL the parts of your body, all the parts of yourself.

Just as our physical form embodies our beliefs, it also holds memories of our life experiences. Pioneers in the field of body/mind therapy, such as Ida Rolf, Moshe Feldenkrais, and Wilhelm Reich, have demonstrated that painful, stressful, and traumatic experiences can leave emotions "frozen" in the tissues of the body. We often shut off our emotions in an attempt to deaden physical pain. Although the physical pain may appear to be gone, the emotions remain trapped inside the body, blocking the natural flow of energy and movement in that area. In this chapter you will learn to "draw" painful events out of your body through words and pictures.

HOW I SEE MYSELF

Create a mental picture of your body as you see and experience it at this time in your life. You might want to actually view your reflection in a full-length mirror. Observe yourself from all angles. Do this for a few minutes.

Draw a picture of yourself. Don't worry about making great "Art" or achieving photographic realism. This is a tool for self-awareness, NOT an assignment in a drawing class.

Study your drawing carefully. Write about what you see in your picture. What does it say about your attitudes and feelings about your body at this time in your life?

Benefits: Here is a chance to deepen your awareness of self by looking at your self-image as expressed in pictures and words.

Note: In doing this exercise you may confront feelings of inadequacy about drawing. Practically all of my students and clients report nervousness and anxiety when asked to draw something recognizable, especially the human form. I hear phrases such as "I can't draw a straight line," or "I don't have any talent," or "I'm not artistic." If you have similar reactions to drawing, consider this as just another experience in which you are trying something new. It's common to become nervous or fearful about the outcome. This includes anything from learning how to ski to starting a new job or visiting a strange city. Observing your reactions to the new and unknown will give you valuable information about your self. This experience can help you break through creative blocks about drawing.

ME AND MY BODY

Interview your body and write it out like the script for a play, as follows:

> ME: Hello, body, I'd like to have a talk and find out more about you.
>
> BODY: O.K. What do you want to know?
>
> ME: (Etc., etc.)

Use two hands and two different colors: one for "me" and another for "body." Use your dominant hand for "me" and your non-dominant hand for your body or body part.

Here are some sample questions to use in your interview:

> How is your health at this time? Do you have any illnesses or problems? Addictions or compulsions? If so, do you have anything to say about it? (If you are receiving treatment or medication ask the next question.) How do you feel about the treatment you are receiving? How do you feel about the practitioner (M.D., etc.)?

> How do you feel about nutrition right now? Am I feeding you enough? Too much? Am I giving you food and beverages that make you healthy? Am I feeding you at the right times and in ways that are truly nourishing for you?

> How do you feel about physical activity and exercise? Are you getting enough? Too much? Is it the right kind? What kind do you like best? What kind do you need at this time?

> How do you feel about rest? Are you getting enough? Too much? Do you sleep well and wake up refreshed? During waking hours do you feel tense or relaxed? Are there particular situations associated with tension? With relaxation? What do you like to do for rest and relaxation?

> How do you feel about your appearance at this time? Your weight? Your posture? Particular body parts? How do you feel about the way

I dress and groom you? Are there any other things you'd like to tell me about?

At the end of the interview, thank your body for sharing with you and for all it does for you. Tell it you are doing this program in well-being in order to be able to better love and care for it.

Benefits: This interview is intended to help you get in closer touch with unconscious feelings and thoughts that live in your body. It can help you identify conflicts between "you" (your ego-self) and the physical/emotional aspect of your being.

PHOTOBIOGRAPHY

Find as many photographs of yourself as you can that were taken at different times in your life. Hopefully your collection includes pictures of you as an infant, child, adolescent, and adult.

Lay the photos out in chronological order from left to right. Study them very carefully. Notice the changes you see there. Observe how your body has changed. Notice the various moods, attitudes, posture, and personal expression. Observe the different clothing and settings. Write your observations down in chronological order.

Benefits: This exercise is designed to help you see how changeable your physical form is. It shows the connection between life situation, self-image, and physical form. Sometimes it is even hard to recognize yourself in the photos because you have changed so much that you do not feel like the same person. You are in charge of your body and there are things you can change if you so choose.

AUTO-BODY-OGRAPHY

Write a brief autobiography of your body or any particular part which is significant to you at this time. Don't think about it or premeditate what you will write. Let the words flow "off the top of your head." Experiment with writing it as a poem. Don't worry about rhyming or form. Just allow the feelings and memories to come out quickly and spontaneously without judging your writing style. You might limit yourself to five minutes so that you don't have time to preplan or edit too much.

Read what you've written and, using your non-dominant hand, write down any feelings that come up.

Benefits: Here is an opportunity to look back on all the physical changes and varieties of experience you've had at different times in your life. It can also help you get in touch with the programming you had regarding your physical form from family, teachers, friends, and society. It can further clarify how you feel about your body at this time in your life.

BODY HISTORY

Make a Body History Chart like the one shown below. List your most memorable physical experiences, such as: significant body changes, weight gain or loss, pregnancy, mastering a new physical skill, illnesses, accidents, or surgery. Make your list in chronological order. Write down how you felt physically and emotionally at the time.

Choose the most significant experience for you. Write about it. You might create a poem or short story in which you describe your physical sensations and your emotional feelings at the time of the event. Writing it in the first person, present tense will give your writing and the reliving of it a greater sense of immediacy.

Reread your account of the experience and, with your non-dominant hand, write down any reaction you have *now* to what happened *then*.

Benefits: When we release old, locked-up feelings through creative expression there is often a physical release as well. If really strong feelings come to the surface as a result of doing the Body History, then turn to the next chapter and do some of the body release exercises or choose one of your own favorite forms of physical release.

BODY HISTORY CHART

Year	Memorable Experience	How I Felt at the Time	
		Physically	*Emotionally*
1956	Earaches.	Horribly painful. Unbearable.	Overwhelmed. Want mom's protection.
1960	Hit in eye with mud clot.	Shock. Pain. Overwhelmed.	Terrified. Afraid I will go blind.
1962	Slipped on hamper and cut calf on metal clip.	Invaded. Body exposed, cut open. Shots, stitches.	Cheated. Vulnerable. Victim.
1963	Cut hand with knife while carving.	Exposed. Body is very vulnerable.	Angry for having scarred my body.
1964	Made all-star team as centerfielder.	Accomplished and capable.	Confident and proud.
1965	Had cyst removed from right knee in emergency room. No anesthesia.	Sickened. Feel blood roll down my leg and pull of the scalpel.	Vulnerable and exposed. Fear.
1966	Second surgery to remove enlarged cyst from knee. Anesthesized.	Humiliated. Orderly shaves leg and pubic hair. Great pain and stiffness for a month.	Disabled. Hobbled. Frustrated.
1970	Auto accident. Jammed knee into glove compartment and broke windshield with head.	Tremendous force smashes into my body. Shaken up and battered. Very sore.	Shock. Check to see if I am still all there. Angry at driver.

BODY HISTORY CHART (Continued)

Year	Memorable Experience	How I Felt at the Time	
		Physically	*Emotionally*
1970	Auto accident. Thrown out of overturning car and over embankment.	Unconscious for 12 hours. Very beaten up and sore. Stitches in face and head. Black eyes. Lucky to be alive.	Cool. Defiant. Embarrassed at appearance. Angry at driver.
1971	Impacted wisdom teeth removed.	Unbearable pain. Bruised jaws. Take lots of pain killers.	Frustrated, angry. Impatient. At end of my rope.
1973	Accidental overdose of medicine for diarrhea in Mexico.	Intense pain and cramping. Leave body, think I'm dying. See white light and slowly come back to consciousness.	Peaceful, happy, and thankful for experience. Lose fear of death.
1973	Learned hatha yoga and meditation.	Poised, calm, confident, balanced, coordinated, fluid.	Serene, peaceful.
1980	Sciatica problems. Stiff neck and back.	Tight, inflexible, pained.	Vulnerable, limited, aging, bound.

| 1985 | Auto accident. Whiplash. Car totaled. | Overloaded. Nervous. Motor coordination impaired. Not sure of myself physically. Numbness. | Shock, anger, rage, feel victimized. Very vulnerable. Ineffectual. Powerless. |
| 1986 | Learned forms of movement therapy and awareness. | Balanced. Poised. Fluid. Strong. Integrated. | Glued back together. Capable. Thankful. Hopeful. |

REMOVAL OF CYST FROM KNEE 1965
(Written with nondominant hand)

I am pissed off that they didn't put me to sleep! And they didn't even give me a private room. Guess the emergency room was cheaper. He still screwed it up and I had to have another operation. Probably was just something in my diet. Now I've got this big scar. They should have got it right the first time. Now I had to use crutches twice. No fun. Probably that's what's wrong with my right hip.

DO LIKE AND DON'T LIKE

Stand in front of a full-length mirror and look at your reflection. Take plenty of time and look at yourself carefully from as many angles as possible. If you don't have a mirror handy, create a mental picture of your entire body.

Now ask yourself:

Which body parts DO I like? Which body parts DON'T I like? First locate the body parts you DO LIKE. Place your hands on each of these areas as you locate them in your mind. Let yourself feel any physical sensations that are happening in each body part as you touch it and focus your attention there. Also, feel any emotions connected with these body parts.

Repeat this with the body parts you DON'T LIKE.

Using the BODY MAP in Chapter Two, color in the areas of your body you DO LIKE and the areas you DON'T LIKE. Choose contrasting colors. For the DO LIKE parts, use colors that you associate with acceptance and love. For the DON'T LIKE parts, use colors that symbolize dislike and unacceptance.

On another page make two columns with the headings: DO LIKE and DON'T LIKE. Then complete each list based on the inventory you just did in your visualization and BODY MAP (see example below). After each item on your DON'T LIKE list, write in the names or initials of people who established or reinforced these negative beliefs in your mind. It may have also been societal values as reflected in advertising and other media which set up an "ideal" body image in your mind. By comparing your *real* body with the "ideal" you may have concluded that you were inadequate, ugly, too fat, too thin, etc. The result is a negative self-image.

DO LIKE	DON'T LIKE	Who taught me to dislike this part?
Hair	Neck	Fashion models in pictures
Face	Fingernails	Mother, nail fashions
Torso	Legs	Mother, other kids
Breasts		
Arms		
Feet		

Benefits Here is a tool for assessing your attitudes about your body by being specific and pinpointing the areas about which you have strong attitudes (positive and negative). In tracing your negative associations back to their early sources, you can see how your self-deprecating attitudes were LEARNED. In later exercises you'll learn how to uproot negative beliefs and cultivate positive ones of your choice.

BODY CONVERSATION

Choose a part of your body that you dislike. Have a written dialogue with it. Write the dialogue out as you would the script for a play. Using your dominant hand, tell the body part how you feel about it. With your non-dominant hand, let the body part respond and tell you how IT feels and why. Find out what it wants from you. You might also want to color in that body part on the BODY MAP or draw a freehand picture of it.

Remember to avoid being critical of the child-like, non-dominant hand. Let it come out in its painfully slow, sluggish, unconventional way, for in its labored efforts lie kernels of truth and revelation.

Benefits: The "judge" that sits in your critical mind and directs "put downs" to your body is usually quite vocal. Your body becomes a battlefield for your destructive criticism. This form of dialogue allows your true feelings to assert themselves in the face of self-judgment. By being able to confront the conflict between feelings and mental judgments, you gradually start to heal the split and become whole.

DIALOGUE WITH HAIR

The following dialogue, written by one of my women students, is a very touching and revealing example of her confrontation between "self-judgment" and her "hair."

ME: I don't like you.

HAIR: I don't like you either.

ME: I wish you were easier for me to manage.

HAIR: I would be—if you knew how.

ME: What's there to know? I try in every way to have you cut properly, groomed properly, combed properly.

HAIR: I like being natural. I don't like haircuts or permanents, which I've been getting for over 30 years. I hate permanents. They stink—they make me fat—I like to be skinny. They make me feel puffy and sometimes frizzy. I look and feel awful with a perm. And those dye jobs—yuk—I hate dye. It's not good for my soil. Sometimes it burns. Why are you trying to change my color? Don't you like my natural look? I wish you'd accept me for what I am. I think I'm beautiful—I wish you thought the same.

ME: I'm trying to change you to suit me better. I guess I can't accept you the way you are. I still feel that you're ugly. You don't look like other people's hair. You only look and feel good when you're freshly washed, and then I can't manage you. Yes, you look beautiful and shiny but your style is pathetic. You don't look the way I'd like you to look. Other people have such nice hair, manageable hair. You've always been a problem to me—as far back as I can remember. Mama had someone (Mrs. C.) perm you since I was little. She couldn't do anything with you either. She also couldn't do anything with her own hair. She still can't even set her own hair. If she can't have someone do it (which she usually doesn't), then it doesn't get done and usually looks horrible. Getting back to you.

HAIR: *We're back to the same subject of acceptance—I wish you could accept me the way I am. I would behave much better if you could. I know it must be hard because you've been programmed with a lot of negative feedback. You've heard it so long and so much and at such an early age that it's going to take a lot to relax with me. Please try to relax with me and I will try to do the same with you. I do love you deep down and think that you're a beautiful, honest, and sincere person and I want to love you more, if only you'd let me.*

(My eyes started tearing at this point.)

ME: You bring tears to my eyes. I really love you too, but somehow I've felt that I was doing the right thing. I saw it as a problem and therefore I've tried to fix the problem. Evidently I've been trying to fix the wrong thing. I'll think more about our discussion today and come up with some workable solution for both of us. I'm glad we talked.

HAIR: *So am I.*

After doing this dialogue, my student stopped using heavy chemicals on her hair, changed her hair style and methods of grooming. As result, she looked many years younger.

OLD AND NEW

Make a chart like the one shown below. List your negative beliefs about your body in the column headed OLD BELIEFS. In the center column, labeled NEW BELIEFS, rewrite each belief as a positive one in the present tense.

OLD BELIEFS	NEW BELIEFS	ACTION
My neck and back will always be a problem.	My neck and back are becoming stronger and more flexible each day.	Take walks, do movement work, breathing and relaxation. Think strong and flexible. See it.
My feet don't support me properly.	My feet are strong, flexible and able to support me in a balanced manner.	Be conscious of how I stand and move, foot placement and weight distribution. Walk every day.
My right sacroiliac joint is weak and I can't rely on it for support.	My sacroiliac joints are becoming stronger and more balanced.	Stop worrying, be free-spirited and spontaneous. Move ahead, walk.
My chest, shoulders and rib cage are tight and constricted.	My chest and rib cage move freely and work well with the other parts of my body.	Breathe, live and take chances. Laugh and do funny things.
My vision is poor.	My vision is steadily improving as I relax the tension in the muscles around my eyes.	Relax. It's OK to see the world as it is. Do eye exercises. Let love flow through my eyes.

Have a dialogue with each body part listed in your OLD BELIEFS column. Ask each body part what it wants you to do to help it express the NEW BELIEF. In the third column, labeled ACTION, write down specifically what you will do to put the NEW BELIEF into effect.

Each time you write down what you will do for the body part, visualize yourself expressing the NEW BELIEF. Picture and feel your body being the way you want it to be.

Note: If your list of negative beliefs is long, focus on just one body part at a time.

Benefits: This exercise can help you consciously choose your own belief system about your body, rather than unconsciously accepting beliefs that were programmed into your mind long ago.

WHAT I SEE IS WHAT I GET

If you are not completely satisfied with your physical form, ask yourself:

How would I like to see, feel and experience my body?

Picture the image of your physical form the way you would like to be. Visualize yourself in everyday activities in this new form. Imagine how you feel, move, dress, and express yourself. Be very concrete about your visualization. In your imaginary scenes, feel the tactile sensations, see the objects and people, hear the sounds, and smell the odors. Sense the way you are moving and being in this new physical form. See how you are be-having toward others. See how they are reacting to you.

Draw a picture of how you would like to be physically. It might be a visually representational picture or an abstract impression of how you'd like to feel. Write positive statements as if the drawing could talk.

Benefits: This exercise can help you learn to visualize more clearly. This is a very important skill if you want to manifest your wishes. The use of visual imagery is an ancient technique in the healing arts and creative endeavors.

Peace & contentment

CHAPTER FOUR

Self-Care: Nurturing
Body, Mind, Spirit

Self-care means listening to all your needs—physical, emotional, mental, and spiritual—and fulfilling those needs. It means living a balanced life in harmony with all parts of yourself. It requires that you discover the ways in which you deny and neglect yourself.

You are not taking care of yourself unless you know and meet your own needs. One way to avoid self-care is to expect others to do it for you. You hand over your power and responsibility to others. When they don't give you what you want, you feel disappointed and resentful. This creates a no-win situation. When you finally learn that self-care begins and ends with you, you no longer demand sustenance and happiness from others.

Another way people often avoid self-care is to take care of others and neglect their own needs, all in the name of love. Self-neglect, masquerading as sacrifice or duty, leads to feelings of martyrdom and eventually rage ("After all I've done for you, how could you. . . ."). If you are taking good care of yourself, you can truly love and serve others from a place of fullness.

The ancient teachings of both East and West have admonished us to "Know thyself." This chapter contains exercises for paying attention to and nourishing your whole being. It includes activities focused on eating and drinking, since physical nourishment is a metaphor for emotional and spiritual nurturance. You will be examining attitudes and behavior related to food, drink, and other substances. You will then be given tools for creating balance in your life on a daily basis.

The most powerful method I know for learning self-care is to find the Nurturing Parent Within and heal your Inner Child through loving, supportive communication. This kind of inner dialogue with the Family Within is at the heart of many methods of therapy, including Gestalt, Transactional Analysis, and Voice Dialogue. This host of inner characters (or sub-personalities) also corresponds with the archetypes of Jungian psychology. Through drawings and dialogues with both hands, you will embrace and integrate your Inner Parent and Inner Child.

NURTURING THE CHILD WITHIN

This is a dialogue between your Vulnerable Child (who feels weak, frightened, upset) and your Inner Nurturing Parent (who gives comfort and support). The Nurturing Parent writes with your dominant hand and asks the child what it wants and needs. Let the Inner Child write with your non-dominant hand and tell exactly what it's feeling, what's missing in the relationship, and what to do about it. Let your Nurturing Parent build trust by telling the Inner Child how it will fulfill the Child's requests.

Whenever you are feeling upset, sit down and let your Vulnerable Child write its feelings out with your non-dominant hand. With your dominant hand, let your Nurturing Parent respond with love and encouragement. This is an excellent exercise to do whenever you are feeling discontented or confused. Often, it is at these times that your Inner Child is feeling either ignored or criticized by your Inner Parent.

Benefits: This exercise gives you a chance to recognize openly the feelings that are often associated with denial, distress, and pain. It also lets you DO something about these feelings by activating the opposite aspect of your personality, the strong, nurturing side. Instead of only seeking support from outside, you can find it within and thereby reduce your demands upon others. The end result is greater self-reliance and wholeness. Also, if you learn to nurture yourself, you can give to others with a feeling of abundance from a truly generous spirit.

What do you want Lil?

I jus want you to like me and love me
and be with
me. Don't
forget me.
You get busy
all the
times +
forget
I'm
here.
You go
run around.
Sometimes you go
with me.
Yeah but lot
of times
yor forget me + I feel dead + numb + sad + lonely + I wants to cry + die. Then I get mad + frustrated + SICK + TIRED. hopeless + helpless, + I want to give up.

DIALOGUE WITH INNER CHILD

Right Hand: What do you want, Lil?

Left Hand: *(Inner Child, whose name is Lil): I jus want you to like me and love me and be with me. Don't forget me. You get busy all the times & forget I'm here. You go run around.*

Right Hand: Sometimes you go with me.

Left Hand: *Yeah, but lot of times you forget me & I feel dead & numb & sad & lonely and I wants to cry & die. Then I get mad & frustrated, hopeless & helpless & I want to give up. SICK & TIRED.*

What I want to do is rest & sleep & not do so much. I like to play with fun people, to go out for dinner, go to movies, go for walks, go out with boys that laugh & are light. Mostly I want you to love me.

DIALOGUE BETWEEN INNER CHILD AND INNER PARENT
Inner Child italics; Inner Parent regular

I want to play. She doesn't let me play. She works too much.

I want to be happy inside. I like to dance & play dolls. I need a friend I can be a child with. I miss being a kid. You know how much I like dolls. You need to let go of the adult and let me shine in your life. I am the real you. Happy, carefree. Do some silly things. Sing. You like to sing. Dance for God. It frees your inner soul.

I want a new dress & shoes and go for walks on the beach. I like balloons and ice cream. I don't want you to work at that job anymore. It makes me sick. My stomach hurts.

Who do you want to play with?

I like Julie. She's my favorite. We pretend we're sisters. I don't want to play with my real sister.

Why?

She's mean. She wants me to do things her way. Don't like that.

Who else would you like to play with?

Edward—he doesn't know it yet but I really like him. Wait til he sees me now. Let me shine for him.

(Nurturing Parent): Mommy loves you very much. I will always take care of you.

I love you. Take me to the beach & buy me a balloon.

I will let you sing and dance more.

Yes. It will make me happy. When I dance I feel close to God. That's what makes me happy. Being close to God. Joy—Joy—Joy from God. Happiness gives me joy.

Would you like new friends?

I just want Julie to play with. She understands my childness. She makes me happy.

What can I do to help the child play & come alive?

Draw, paint, sing, be close to God. Don't worry so much. God is working just fine in your life. Be still & listen. He's the best teacher.

FOOD: A FREE ASSOCIATION

Your attitudes and habits concerning food are shaped in early childhood by your parents or other care-givers. If you have unhealthy eating or drinking patterns and want to change them, it is important to get to the root of these attitudes. Once you uncover them, you then have an opportunity to change them. As long as they lie buried in the unconscious, you have no free choice. The negative attitudes continue to breed negative behavior.

Write down the word *food* (or any other word that means "physical nourishment" to you). Then write in free-association any words that come to mind. Write quickly, off the top of your head. Don't think or ponder over it too much. Let the words flow freely. Let each word trigger the next in a chain reaction.

Afterward, look over the list and write down any observations you have. Also, write out any feelings you had while making your list of words. Other thoughts or feelings on the theme of food, eating, or nurturance may come to you. Write them down. This can be in prose or even poetic form.

Benefits: This exercise can help you explore your unconscious attitudes about food and nourishment. It is especially helpful to deal with these attitudes if eating or drinking have become a problem area for you (as in the case of overeating, alcoholism, bulimia, etc.).

FOODS AND MOODS

Write about eating and drinking. Which settings or circumstances do you prefer? Which ones do you dislike? Which people do you enjoy eating with? Why? Describe a favorite eating experience: the setting, people, food, and feelings you had at the time.

What is the significance of food in your life? Is eating related to any particular emotions? What about drinking? Do you crave particular foods or beverages when you are in certain moods? If so, what are they? If possible, observe this pattern *when it happens*, and try to write about it then, or as soon as possible.

What are your favorite foods and beverages? Make a list, using your non-dominant hand. Next to each item on your list, write a word which describes how you *feel* inside when you think of that particular food or drink. Review your list of foods/drinks and feelings and write down any observations you have.

Benefits: Here is an opportunity to become more aware of your attitudes, feelings, and habits concerning nutrition. It can help you understand the deeper, emotional significance food has in your life beyond physical sustenance. These exercises have been very helpful for individuals with problems, such as addictions and compulsions.

Note: If you suffer with substance abuse of any kind (drugs, alcohol, cigarettes, etc.), modify the exercise and focus on the substance in question rather than food.

TUMMY TALKS

Meditate on your digestive system. Sense where everything is. Imagine from memory what happens when you eat. Start with your nose smelling the odor, your eyes seeing the food, and your hand putting it into your mouth. Perceive what happens next, following the food as it travels from one area to another along the digestive system. Don't worry about correct anatomy, simply sense it from your own experience. If it's not clear to you, then actually eat something and follow the process while it's happening.

Draw a picture of your digestive and elimination system. Again, don't be concerned with anatomical correctness. Simply express YOUR experience of these systems in your body.

Let each part of your drawing speak to you. Write down what it says. For instance, what does your mouth say? What does your stomach say? What about your intestines? What foods do they like? Which ones do they dislike? Why? What does each area want in order for it to feel good and be healthy?

Benefits: This exercise is intended to help you get in touch with what your body wants and needs for good health. Often we let our emotions or misguided beliefs about eating control us, rather than listening to the wisdom that lies within us. This exercise can also help you become more aware of the inner workings of your body and can be applied to any other internal system as well.

GETTING UNHOOKED

Make a list of your addictive or compulsive behaviors. This could include overeating, alcoholism, smoking, drug addiction, compulsive sex, over-sleeping, compulsive television viewing, gambling, workoholism, compulsive indebtedness, compulsive shopping, or being in abusive or co-addictive relationships (in which you rescue others and put your own needs last).

Choose one item on the list and focus on it for a specific period of time (four days, a week, a month). Each time the compulsion or overpowering urge comes up, instead of giving in to it do one or more of the following:

1. Draw or write how you feel in your journal.

2. Draw a picture or diagram of your relationship with that substance, behavior, or person.

3. Write a dialogue with your body. Let your body speak through the non-dominant hand. Ask your body how it feels. Tell your body you are helping it overcome the addiction or compulsion. Tell your body what YOU want.

Repeat these exercises as often as you wish, focusing on one item for each period of time. Don't overwhelm yourself by trying to handle too many behaviors at once.

Benefits: Anything you MUST have imprisons you and controls your life to some degree. This exercise can be helpful in openly confronting and handling addictive and compulsive urges. Here, we are dealing with the internal force which allows the addiction to gain power over you. This approach *does not* use punishment, but stresses open communication, understanding, and self-care.

Note: If an addiction has control of your life, find a support system. I recommend the Twelve Step Programs (Alcoholics Anonymous, Alanon, etc.). There's a program for just about any addiction.

EATING PATTERNS

Observe your pattern of eating for at least one week. Notice the following: How did you eat (fast, slow)? What mood were you in when you ate (anxious, distracted, hurried, pressuring yourself)? Where did you eat? What did you eat and how much? How did the food taste? Did you feel satisfied? Each day write down highlights of your observations.

At week's end, look over your observational notes. Write about any reactions you have and any recurring patterns you see.

How would you like things to be in the future regarding your eating and drinking habits? Imagine how it will be, visualize it. Then write your future projection in the *present tense* as if it were already a fact.

Write down what you can do in everyday life to bring about the future projection you just created.

How do you feel about cooking? For yourself? For others? Is cooking related to an expression of love and creativity, or is it a necessary duty that you "have to" do? Write about your attitudes regarding cooking and preparing meals.

Benefits: This exercise encourages you to take a closer look at your behavior and self-nurturing abilities in general. It helps you be specific in documenting your current patterns, observing the negative aspects and projecting more positive ones for the future.

NURTURING ALL OF ME

What do you do to nurture the physical, emotional, mental, and spiritual aspects of your being? Make four lists, one for each category. Under each heading write the people, places, things, and activities in your life that develop that particular aspect. As you write each item down, visualize it and re-experience your enjoyment of it. Really conjure up the sensory impressions of these nurturing elements in your life.

Every day, do something to nurture and develop each of these four aspects of yourself. Write out a daily checklist with a plan of what you intend to do. (See sample on next page.) Write down the activities with your non-dominant hand. At the end of the week, review your list to see how you did.

Benefits: This is a method for becoming aware of and expressing the four aspects of your being and thereby developing your whole self. This technique can help you stay balanced and in alignment, since each part of you is getting positive attention and reinforcement. If you are weak or having problems in any particular aspect, give it extra opportunities to express and develop.

Example:

Monday
Physical: Rollerskate
Emotional: Draw in journal
Mental: Read for an hour, attend lecture
Spiritual: Meditate, read spiritual book

Tuesday
Physical: Take walk at the beach, attend dance class
Emotional: Write about an emotional experience
Mental: Attend a class in writing
Spiritual: Meditate, visit meditation garden

Wednesday
Physical: Ride bike, exercise at home
Emotional: Go to lunch and art museum with friends
Mental: Watch educational video
Spiritual: Attend seminar in spiritual meditation

Thursday
Physical: Exercise at home, doing spontaneous movement to music
Emotional: Play musical instrument or listen to music
Mental: Read
Spiritual: Attend meditation group

Friday:
Physical: Ride bike or take walk
Emotional: Attend play
Mental: Read and write in journal
Spiritual: Meditate

MY NURTURING SELF

Do *Inner Journey* and *Body Mapping I* or *II* (Chapter Two).

Close your eyes and let your "Nurturing Self" speak to any body part that seems to need attention. Let your Nurturing Self tell your body part how much you love and appreciate it and what you will do to help it feel better. Then, using your dominant hand, write these loving messages out in your journal.

Close your eyes and allow your body parts to receive these loving messages. Really feel the tender, loving care as you sense the nurturing messages. Pay special attention to the areas you just communicated with, but also let the message extend to all parts of your body. Feel your body relax, and experience a light, tingling sensation all over—inside and out.

Benefits: This is an excellent way to learn self-care and develop greater sensitivity to your body. It is also a very effective relaxation method, with great benefits for those under stress.

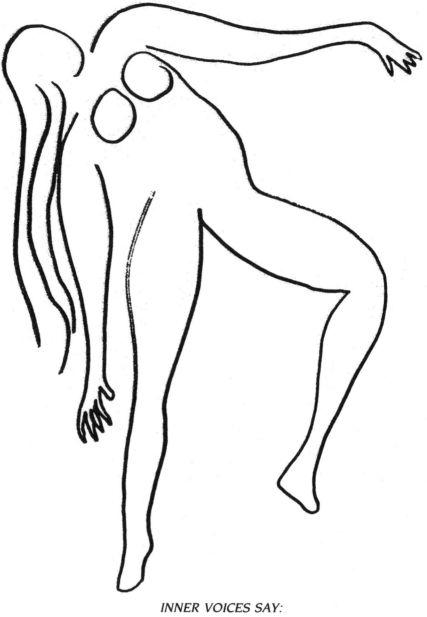

INNER VOICES SAY:
(Written with Non-dominant Hand)

Relax and let me explore and look around and play some new games, invent some new rules or throw the rules away sometimes. Let's just play around and see where it all leads—what have we got to lose?

CHAPTER FIVE

Relaxation and Re-creation

Today we know that chronic stress and tension contribute to the development of disease and pain. Tension is often caused by feelings held in (suppressed) or denied (repressed). The feelings don't go away, however, they simply remain imprisoned in the body as stiffness, discomfort, or disease. In this chapter you will learn some effective and playful ways to release emotional build-up through creative expression. You will be scribbling, doodling to music, drawing, and writing. You need no training or special talent to use the arts for reducing stress. Creative expression is an innate human capability which can be developed or revived at any age.

Relaxation has many benefits beyond simple release of tension. Leaders in the field of holistic health, such as Herbert Benson, M.D., and Joan Borysenko, Ph.D., have written about the beneficial effects of relaxation on the body, especially the immune system. Dr. Benson coined the term, *The Relaxation Response,* and described in detail its physiological benefits, such as a drop in heart rate and blood pressure, slowing down in rate of breathing, and a state of restful mental alertness. By contrast, a high-stress lifestyle often overstimulates the "fight or flight" response, which is necessary when dealing with danger, but destructive when it becomes an habitual coping pattern.

This chapter contains activities designed to help you slow down and relax physically, emotionally, and mentally. You will examine your current activities and priorities to see if you are neglecting your own health in deference to obligations and responsibilities. New tools will then be presented for creating a lifestyle with a healthy regard for your own well-being. The activities in this chapter were designed to help you reduce stress in a light and playful way. You'll have an opportunity to activate the creative right hemisphere of your brain. You'll reawaken the Magical Child within yourself (the part of you which holds the key to imagination and creativity) and learn to enjoy life more fully.

DRAWING YOUR FEELINGS OUT

Choose a color that expresses how you feel right now. Scribble or doodle your feelings out onto the page. Don't try to make a picture or symbol. Simply allow your hand to move about freely on the page. Then switch to your non-dominant hand and do another page of scribbling or doodling that expresses your mood. Continue doing this with either hand until you've gotten your feelings out. Then write a few words to express the feelings.

Alternate: Doodle with your eyes closed so that you can pay more attention to your body sensations and movement while you draw.

Benefits: Here is a way to get out of your rational mind and into your physical sensations and emotional feelings. This activity encourages you to loosen up, play around, let go of some of your inhibitions and restrictions.

HOW DO I FEEL RIGHT NOW? (with Non-dominant hand)

I am reaching and running
searching and creating
diving and hiding
hoping and waiting
climbing and riding
flying and falling
looking and lying
active and confused
sleepy and amused
afraid and crazed
loving and amazed
solid and divided
genius and fool
lost and found
a clinging clown
  desperate saint
a perpetually tamed
  beast with a name

a horror and honor
  god without armor
  dish without bottom

A star with an
  open hand
reaching for motion
  going nowhere often
mask on the run
  sun with legs
a silly face, noble
  mobile
  nubile
  fragile
  tactile
  soul
silenced
  &
roaming
  still

A DANCE ON PAPER

Play some music that expresses your mood. Scribble or doodle to the music. Don't try to draw a picture or representational image. Just let your pen, pencil, or crayon move freely on the paper as though you were dancing. Your drawing will be like the tracks skaters leave on the ice. As you draw be aware of the movement of your arms and shoulders. Let the rhythm fill your entire body.

For relaxation:

Choose music that gives you a feeling of peace and serenity, such as the music of Steve Halpern or Kitaro. Some other suggestions are: *Music for Zen Meditation,* by Tony Scott; *Inside The Taj Mahal* or *Inside The Great Pyramid* by Paul Horn. (See the Discography for more information.)

Alternate 1: Draw with your nondominant hand.

Alternate 2: Before drawing to music, let yourself dance or move to the music with your entire body. Don't worry about dance steps, just let your body move freely to the rhythm of the music. Close your eyes and focus on the inner sensations of the movement. Let your body tell you how it wants to move. Let it naturally release tension, stiffness, and stress.

Benefits: This activity brings together the three forms of expression: art, music, and dance. It helps you relax and explore many ways to release feelings and energy stored up inside.

TENSION AND RELAXATION

Draw a picture of *tension*. This can be an abstract design or doodle. It can be a symbolic portrait or cartoon of yourself in a state of tension.

Let your tension speak, and write down what it says. Let it tell you how it feels, what causes it, and what you can do about it.

Lie down or sit in a comfortable chair. Starting at your feet, tense them up as much as possible and then let go completely. Tense and relax your feet, legs, and torso. Then tense and relax your shoulders, neck, arms, and hands. Repeat this with your head and face. Enjoy being relaxed.

After you have experienced relaxing fully, draw a picture of *relaxation*. This can be an abstract design, a doodle, or a picture of yourself being relaxed.

Benefits: This activity increases your awareness of the difference between relaxation and tension. Often we become so habituated to tension we are unaware of it until its effects show up in particular parts of the body. This exercise will help you experience your tension level, and provide a means to relax quickly and effectively.

What do you feel about work?
Too much—too much
cried the Doormouse
I need more help—I don't
want to lead alone
I want others—I can't
carry the load

Left Hand: *What do you feel about work?*
               Too much—too much
               cried the Doormouse
               I need more help—I don't
               want to lead alone
               I want others—I can't
               carry the load

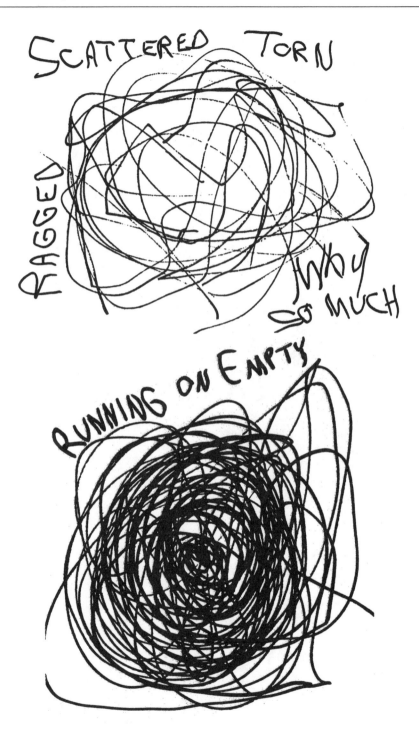

SLOWING DOWN

Write your name in your journal, but do it *as slowly as you possibly can*. For instance, take five minutes to write your first name. You might then go on to write a brief relaxing message to yourself, such as: "Slow down" or "Take it easy" or "Relax." Again, do this in slow motion so that the pen is barely moving.

Repeat the above activity, but this time use your non-dominant hand.

Scribble or doodle in slow motion. Take several minutes to make a line or shape. Let your hand wander aimlessly around the page as you draw. Consciously slow down as much as possible. It is helpful to do one of the other relaxation meditations first, so that you are reinforcing the intention to relax through a variety of methods.

Repeat with your non-dominant hand.

Benefits: This is an excellent exercise when you feel hyperactive or nervous. It is very difficult to remain "speedy" when writing or drawing in slow motion. This kind of meditative writing and drawing has a self-hypnotic effect and calms the mind and body. However, it is important that you write messages which are positive and relaxing. The *Tension and Relaxation* activity earlier in this chapter would be a good prelude to this exercise.

REST AND RELAXATION

When rest and relaxation are missing from your life, some of the symptoms are stress, short temper, emotional upset, inefficiency, forgetfulness, fatigue, aches, and pains. If you are neglecting this essential component of good health, it is important to take inventory and make some changes.

Do the *Breathing Meditation* from Chapter Two and repeat this visualization with your eyes closed. What do you do for rest and relaxation? Make three lists. *People, Places,* and *Activities* that are relaxing to you. Take your time to complete these lists and be as thorough as possible.

Read your lists over. Now think of some new ways of relaxing. Add these to the appropriate lists.

Write about some ways you can make your life more restful and relaxing. Outline methods for actually applying these ideas in your everyday life. Be practical and specific. Implement your plans, and then check back in a few days to see how you're doing.

When you're stressed, take time to do this *Beautiful Place Meditation*—remember a beautiful place you have visited, one in which you felt calm and peaceful. Picture the beautiful place in your mind's eye. Look all around you and take in the surroundings through all your senses. See the objects, shapes, colors. Feel the textures. Smell the odors. Hear the sounds around you. Sense the general atmosphere. Now close your eyes, picture the beautiful place, and allow yourself to relax fully and enjoy this environment.

Benefits: This is an opportunity to reflect upon your current life pattern and how you replenish your energy and restore yourself. It is also an excellent way to let daydreaming help you achieve a centered and peaceful state of being.

WHERE THE TIME GOES

Make a list of all your life activities (see below). Itemize the activities you are currently involved in and write down the approximate number of hours in a typical week you devote to each activity.

Activities

Sleeping	Socializing
Eating	Recreation
Food preparation, shopping, etc.	Physical exercise
Personal grooming	Hobbies
Household maintenance	Entertainment
Commuting, Traveling	Education
Working, Studying	Spiritual practices

Draw a large circle and divide it into pie-shaped pieces representing each item on your list. The size of the piece is determined by the percentage of time you devote to that activity.

Check your priorities at the present time. If you'd like to make changes, make a new list showing how you would LIKE to spend your time, then draw a new circle and fill it in, reflecting your new priorities.

Make a one-week calendar and fill in the new activities, indicating the amount of time devoted to each. Then write about how you will implement the changes in your everyday life. Give special attention to health-oriented and self-care activities.

Benefits: Here is a good tool for seeing your current priorities and then planning your life more consciously, with specific needs and goals in mind. This will help you take better charge of your time instead of feeling like a helpless victim of the clock. Time is like money: you can spend it any way YOU choose. It is really up to you.

WHERE THE TIME GOES

December 1

The month of November disappeared—vanished—when I wasn't look-ing. Where did it go? I can't remember a month ever passing so quickly. I was so involved in proposals and budgets and deals and presentations that, before I could turn around, the days were gone. It seems like barely two weeks ago that I wrote my monthly list of goals. And *yesterday* it was already "the day of reckoning" to see if I'd reached my goals. Some I had, others I hadn't. Some I dropped intentionally because I'd change my mind. Anyway, it all goes by so very quickly.

Sometimes I wish I could just slow time down, get all the clocks to run more slowly. I guess the only thing I can do is slow down inside. Calm down, even out—take it easy. But it's hard because I love variety and excitement and juggling several balls in the air at once. It's just a problem of staying centered in the midst of throwing all the balls up and catch-ing them over—and over—and over—and over (oops! dropped one)—and over—and over again.

I need more nature: more sunsets, more oceans, more trees, more sky, more flowers, more beauty. . . . Next week I'm going up north . . . a get-away. I just need some uninterrupted time—with no phones ringing, no demands, no breaks in my attention. It's just so draining to have inter-ruptions of the flow and concentration all the time. I need to use my answering machine more often when I'm home. I'm aware that I feel frag-mented a lot because of interruptions.

I need to hold certain pieces of time sacred, private, holy—"no trespass-ing," "do not disturb." I remember Jane's story of her mother (who had thirteen children) with her "do not disturb" bonnet. When she wanted to be left alone, she wore her bonnet. If she hadn't done that, the poor lady probably would have gone insane, committed murder, or taken to the bottle.

How do we carve out some private space and time? How do we guard our souls and keep watch over our inner selves? How do we protect our essential beings from encroachment by the noisy buzz of the daily rou-tines we call our lives?

I suppose these are some of the questions religions try to answer. They create sabbaths and special holy days and retreats and rituals and the like. They put them on a yearly calendar and guard those days and seasons from being eaten up alive by mundane "duties," jobs, and other "have to's."

DAILY TREATS

Make a list of special treats for you to give to yourself. You may want to dialogue with your Inner Child again and ask it what it needs. You can ask the Child to draw a picture (with your non-dominant hand), showing the "treats" it wants.

Each day, give yourself *at least* one special treat. Plan your treats at the beginning of the day or week. Write them down on your calendar and *do them.*

> Saturday: Sleep in, breakfast in bed, take a bubble bath, walk in the park
>
> Sunday: Play tennis with Nancy
>
> Monday: Buy that book I've been wanting
>
> Tuesday: Go out to dinner and a movie with friends

Each week add more treats.

Benefits: This exercise focuses on self-appreciation. It is intended to help you identify things you like to do. It encourages you to be good to yourself by scheduling treats into your calendar, instead of leaving them only to happenstance.

A DAY OFF

Plan a day off. Plan to do things you enjoy but don't normally do. Find activities which are relaxing, inspiring, energizing, etc. If possible, do not work or do chores on that day. Let this truly be a day off, a mini-vacation from routine and duty. Spend some time during the day relieving any tension you are carrying. Try a massage, hot tub, sun bath, etc. Write or draw out your plans.

Take your day off and do the things you planned.

Write about your day off. What was it like? Did you do the things you planned? Were you resistant? Did you fill up the day with chores and other routine activities?

Plan another day off. Let this one be different in some way. List the things you want to experience. You may even want to plan a spontaneous day with no planning. Just let yourself relax and flow with your feelings on that particular day. Be good to yourself!

Repeat the "day off" exercise on a regular basis, i.e., once a week, a month, etc.

Benefits: Here is an opportunity to set aside your routine and treat yourself to activities you truly enjoy. It is a way of saying, "I love you" to yourself. This is an effective method for finding out what makes you feel good and then giving yourself those things.

Note: If you think you can't take an entire "day off," then start with a half day.

REFLECTIONS ON EMPTY SPACE AND TIME

April 7

It's hard sometimes to leave empty space and time for nothing. Just nothing-ness. No plans, no schemes, no activities, no goals, no achievements, no tasks—just nothing. A block of uninterrupted time to lie around, lounge, daydream—do nothing in particular—live by no schedule or agenda . . . just a hunk of time with which to do nothing.

I say it's hard to let this happen because I'm so accustomed to doing, going, accomplishing, planning, getting "there," getting back, getting ready to go some other where. Preparing for this or that. Cleaning up, organizing, communicating. I don't realize how busy I am until I stop—to do NOTHING!

I wonder about why it's hard to leave open time for nothing. What happens when I do that? What "happens" in the nothing space? Maybe it's not so much what will "happen" as it is what will "be"—me. And that means stopping to be with myself, my feelings, my memories, my thoughts, my urges, my dreams—all that inner world of me. . . .

MOVING RIGHT ALONG

What are your attitudes about exercise and physical activity? Write about them. Are you involved in any regular form of exercise, such as sports, running, walking, dance, yoga, martial arts? If so, write about the significance of these activities in your life. Actually describe what you do and how you feel when you're doing it. Draw pictures of the activity.

If you're not getting enough exercise, then write about that. What is inhibiting or limiting you from physical activity and enjoyment?

How can you enjoy your body more? Write a conversation with your body and ask it what it would like. What activities does it enjoy most? When does it feel best? What other things can you do to make it feel good? What about its preference in clothing, grooming, foods, etc.? Write your conversation with your body as if it were a script for a play. It is preferable to write or print what the body says, using the non-dominant hand.

Benefits: In this activity you are encouraged to approach exercise as enjoyable and revitalizing, rather than "unpleasant medicine" you MUST take because it's good for you. As with strict dieting, a duty-bound attitude usually creates resistance and rebellion and is self-destructive.

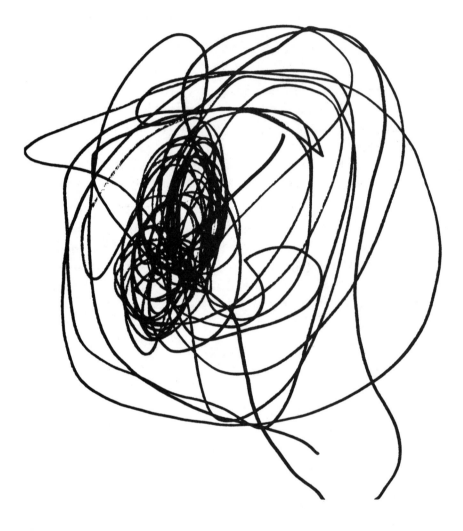

TIME TO PLAY

The Playful and the Magical Child are aspects of your personality that are crucial for happiness and well-being. It is the Playful Child in you who knows how to really have fun, be spontaneous, silly, and enjoy itself. It is the Magical Child who loves to explore, be imaginative, and express itself creatively.

What do you like to do for enjoyment? Make a list of your favorite "fun" activities. Let your Playful Child write this list by using your non-dominant hand.

Check over the list and see which items you have neglected lately. Do you want to revive them? If so, write about how to do that.

With your non-dominant hand, let your Playful Child draw pictures of how it wants to play.

With your non-dominant hand, let your Magical Child write a list of all the ways it expresses creativity, adventuresomeness, or inventiveness in all areas of your life. This can include solving mechanical problems, redesigning and accessorizing your home environment, creating a new computer program, surviving in nature, traveling in a foreign country, or adjusting to relocation.

With your dominant hand, write about all the creative abilities *you want to develop*. With your non-dominant hand, draw a picture of your Magical Child and write a dialogue with it. Ask it how it wants to express itself creatively in any area of your life.

Benefits   Here is an opportunity to enhance your life through pleasurable and creative activities. Nurture yourself by being in touch with the fun-loving child that still lives within you and wants to come out and play. You can also unleash the joy of hidden creativity by tapping into your Magical Child.

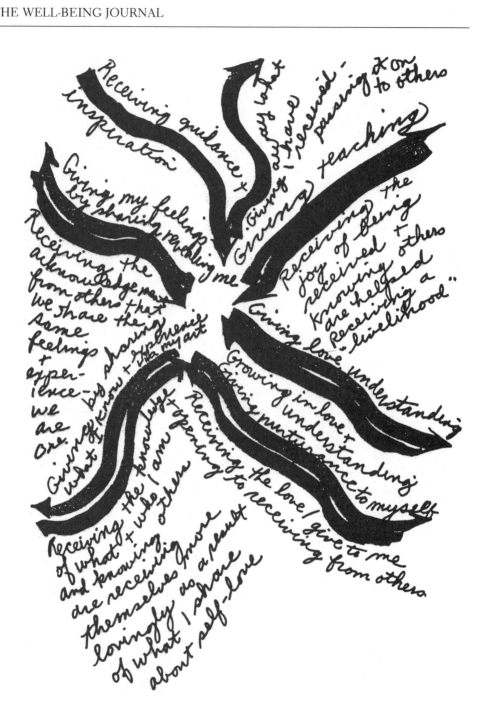

CHAPTER SIX

Supportive Relationships

Supportive, nurturing relationships begin with yourself. Just as you pat your friends on the back and encourage them to go for their dreams, you need to do the same for *you*. The great enemy of supportive relationships is the judgmental mind. When your mind is filled with destructive thoughts and beliefs, it becomes an enemy of your emotions, your body, and your life. In describing the relationship of the mind and body, the Bhagavad Gita (an ancient Hindu scripture) says: "The body is a field." Your thoughts are like seeds planted in that field. If you sow negative thoughts, you reap negative fruits in your body and in your life. If you sow positive thoughts, you reap positive fruits. "As you sow, so shall you reap."

This chapter gets you in touch with that inner voice which supports you even in difficult times. There are techniques for helping you cultivate self-esteem through creative expression, and to communicate love more openly to yourself and others.

Self-love is the basis of all healthy relationships. It enables you to create a strong network of love and support. However, our society breeds competition, distrust, and alienation. This causes stress and feelings of isolation, which are especially devastating when illness or crisis hit. Many activities in this chapter will help you cultivate your personal support system. This involves identifying those people with whom you have a mutually nourishing relationship, and acknowledging their value in your life. It is also important to recognize those people with whom you are in conflict.

This chapter includes techniques for exploring attitudes about sexuality and about being male or female. You'll learn ways to balance the male and female within, and strengthen loving relationships with others. And you will experience the healing power of forgiveness for people with whom you have been in conflict. Hopefully you'll come to understand how your connection with the outside world is a mirror of your relationship with yourself.

MY OWN BEST FRIEND

You can make friends with your mind by guiding and monitoring your internal chatter, especially the critical thoughts you have about yourself. Write down your current negative beliefs about yourself (as shown below). Include self-judgments that you keep private, as well as those you communicate to others. Transform each one into a positive affirmation.

Example:

NEGATIVE

I can't write very well.

POSITIVE

My writing is getting better all the time. The more I write the better I get.

Apply this in your everyday life. Each time you think a critical, negative thought about yourself, STOP and consciously replace it with a positive one. When you *say* something negative or cynical about yourself out loud, STOP yourself. Take back what you said and replace it with a positive statement. Ask friends to support you in practicing positive speech, so that you can co-create a more loving, nurturing atmosphere.

Benefits: Negative thoughts and beliefs are self-fulfilling prophecies. If you believe and expect the worst, that's exactly what you'll get. By dwelling on negative thoughts you bring on the very conditions and situations you dread or dislike. Build up a big bank account of positive thoughts and spoken affirmations. Remember, *thought creates form.* So watch your thoughts and words.

THE GIFT OF FRIENDSHIP

Write down the names of all your close friends and loved ones at this time in your life. Visualize each one as you write his or her name.

Choose one person from your list and write about the relationship. What does this person mean to you? What do you give to the relationship? What do you receive from it? How do you show your appreciation to this person? What can you do in the future to show appreciation?

Write a letter to that person, sharing your thoughts and feelings about the value of your relationship. You can send the letter or not, as you choose.

Benefits: Here is a chance to cultivate appreciation and thanks for the friendships and other loving relationships that bless your life. Gratitude and expressions of thanks go a long way toward helping love grow and blossom inside yourself and in your world.

PERSONAL SUPPORT SYSTEM

Who are the people you turn to when you need understanding, honest feedback, encouragement, support, or assistance of any kind? This might include family members, friends, neighbors, co-workers, and professionals who provide special services.

Consider these people as your personal support system. Picture them in your mind's eye and experience the feelings you have about them. Contemplate how each of these people contribute to your life. Also picture the ways in which you support them.

Draw a picture with yourself in the center and the members of your personal support group around you. Next to each person, write in how he or she supports you.

Examine your picture. If you feel a need to strengthen your support system, write down any changes you want to make. Implement these in your everyday life.

Contemplate an "ideal" support network. How does it look? How does it feel to have all the support you need? Draw a picture of your "ideal" support system and then write about it.

Benefits: This is a highly effective means for doing an inventory of personal needs and resources. If your assessment shows that you depend too much on one or two individuals, you may decide to broaden your base of support. Reaching out for assistance when you need it can be extremely empowering. It helps you nourish yourself and build bridges between yourself and others.

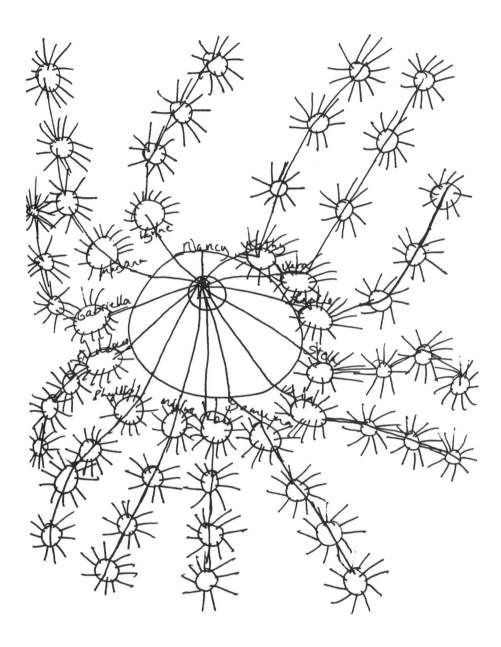

THE HEALING LETTER

Think of someone toward whom you feel anger and resentment. In your journal write a letter of forgiveness for anything you think they've done, said or thought to hurt you. Meditate upon the passage from the Lord's Prayer: ". . . forgive us our trespasses as we forgive those who trespass against us."

Whenever you like, continue this exercise until you've written forgiveness letters to everyone toward whom you bear a grudge or hard feelings of any kind. These letters are not intended to be sent, but meant for you as an exercise in forgiveness. If you wish to communicate directly with someone you've written to in your journal, that is your choice.

Think of all the people you have harmed through negative thoughts, deeds, words, negligence, etc. In your journal write each one a letter asking for forgiveness.

Write a letter of forgiveness to yourself.

Benefits: Here is an opportunity to put the golden rule into practice and to apply that passage from the Lord's Prayer to your life. Individuals who have cured themselves of so-called incurable diseases (such as cancer) have reported that this kind of forgiveness was an essential part of their healing. They shared that anger was a poison that had to be released. Don't forget to let go of the anger toward yourself, too.

PICTURE ME SEXUAL

Draw a picture of your "sexuality," whatever that means to you. Let the drawing unfold spontaneously without planning it.

Look at your drawing for a few minutes and simply observe it without judging it.

Now let the drawing speak in the first person present tense. Use the non-dominant hand to write down what it says.

If you are not happy with your sexuality, ask yourself:

How would I like to feel about my sexuality?

Do a new drawing of how you would like to experience your sexual self. Again, create your own definition of the word "sexual." You may even choose another word. Let the new drawing speak, as in the first part of this exercise.

Benefits: This process gives you a chance to be creative in your understanding and expression of a very powerful and often misunderstood natural force within.

THE FACTS OF LOVE

What are your current attitudes and beliefs about love? About sex? Write them out. Take plenty of time and be thorough.

Have you always held the same attitudes and beliefs about sex? About love? If not, what were your previous attitudes and beliefs? As a child and adolescent, what were you taught about sex (at home, school, church, peer group)? What did you learn about love? Write down your memories.

If there has been a change in your attitudes, values, and beliefs about love and sex, when did it occur? What brought about the change or new awareness? Write about it.

Benefits: In this exercise you are encouraged to sort through all the beliefs, attitudes, and values about sex and love you have been exposed to during your life. You are also invited to clarify what YOU believe at this time in your life, and the relation between your beliefs and life experience.

MALE AND FEMALE

How do you feel about your sex? If you're a man, how do you feel about being in a male body? If you're a woman, how do you feel about being in a female body? Draw it. Write about it.

Exactly what does being a man or woman mean to you in practical terms? What are the limitations and what are the advantages as you experience them? Imagine that you CHOSE to be born the sex you are. What kinds of experiences do you think you wanted by choosing to be a member of your sex?

What are your beliefs about men/women in general? Make two lists. Entitle one: MEN ARE . . . and head the other list: WOMEN ARE . . . Complete each list with your beliefs about each one.

Review your list of beliefs and see if you have any negative or prejudicial attitudes about either or both. Pinpoint the negative beliefs. If you want to change them, do the first exercise in this chapter, *My Own Best Friend.*

Benefits: This exercise is intended to help you examine your underlying beliefs about sex roles, sexual identity, and stereotypes. It can help you uncover prejudices (which may be unconscious) and aid you in developing more positive attitudes toward your own and/or the opposite sex.

THE MARRIAGE WITHIN

Swiss psychologist Carl Jung taught us that within each man there is a woman (called the Anima), and within each woman there is a man (called the Animus). When we recognize and integrate the function of the Anima or Animus in our lives, we experience a sense of wholeness within ourselves, and a true humanity in relationship to others. Once this balance of male/female within is attained, it is then mirrored in our daily life. It enriches and harmonizes existing relationships or helps us create new healthy ones.

Meditate upon the two sides of your personality: the male and female principles. You might think of them as Receptive (feminine, responsive, intuitive) and Active (masculine, logical, goal-oriented). Create your own name for these two principles and write them down as the heading for two columns. In each column write down the qualities you associate with that principle.

Draw a picture of each "character": the male and female within. Using both hands, have a dialogue between the two sides of your personality. Give each side a name and its own color. Choose which hand to use for each personality part based on your own sense of appropriateness. Some people refer to "he" and "she" or male and female names in doing this exercise. Others give them names like "the thinker" and "the dreamer" or "the businessman" and "the artist."

Read over your dialogue and write down any observations that come to you. It is advisable to do this dialogue on a fairly regular basis if you find there is conflict between your male and female sides. They need to get together, so you can live in peace.

Benefits: Here is an opportunity to give a voice to both sides of your personality. It is especially helpful in allowing the non-dominant or suppressed parts of you to speak up. These hidden places within often contain much wisdom and creativity when given a chance to express.

THE INNER MAN

Yea—hey—Here I am! The big wheeler-dealer guy (but I come from the heart, lady). Yeah, I go out and do it with my car and briefcase. I do what it takes to work all day—make a few deals, a few bucks and I come home to the little lady. My wonderful, adoring woman who feeds me passionately with food, sex, humor, caring, nurturing, with wit and charm. She gives me the space to be a man—wanted and needed and loved.

She gives me ideas, laughter, and the solutions to many of my problems. She knows all the right restaurants, books, movies. She relaxes me with meditation and spiritual inspiration. She takes me on quiet walks and we listen to music. She makes me rest and see who I am so I can go out and serve the world—my clients, my customers—and do business with great people and then shovel in the dough.

She makes love for love's sake.

THE INNER WOMAN

Well, I'm not exactly your little lady, but I know what you mean and I take it well. You go out there in your man's cold world of logic, power, money, and sex—you meet interesting people, put deals together that will benefit many. You get the right information out there—the right images—you help the right people and you get paid for it very well. So when you come home, you deserve all the wonderful pleasures that I can provide. I know how to love, nurture, play, laugh, cook, and make merry. I read all the right things and say all the bright and witty things—have hot tubs, massages, long walks and drives. I grow flowers and vegetables. I take refuge in divine love, as you are Shiva and I am Shakti. We cannot separate the one from the other. We are both masters and disciples of the one another. We are the same flame of love.

DIALOGUE WITH MALE AND FEMALE WITHIN
All written with non-dominant hand

July 21

Man: *I'm the man—I know what I want and I get it! I'm powerful, directed. I achieve my goals and sometimes I get dry and tired and ask myself: Is this all there is to life?*

Woman: *I'm the woman. I love beautiful things. I love art and poetry and wonderful clothes. And I wait for things to happen.*

Man: *I make things happen. I'm in charge, responsible.*

Woman: *I like the spontaneous, the unexpected, the surprise. I can give up control, let a higher power run things when I don't know what to do or when he (the inner man) doesn't get what he wants. I turn it over to God. He's rigid, the man is. He gets an idea in his head and if it doesn't turn out exactly the way he wanted it, he gets irritable.*

Man: *I want to be in control. I don't like flakiness.*

Woman: *I don't like flakiness either. But I also face up to things beyond the control of reason.*

Man: *I think you help me with that.*

Woman: *Good. And you help me feel more powerful in achieving tasks and goals, in wanting things for myself. And I still must be in some conflict because I still feel badly that I don't have a male partner (outer relationship) in my life.*

Man: *You have me.*

Woman: *Yes I know. But it's not the same. I can't get to know you . . . as a separate person with a life of your own.*

Man: *But you have good friends who are men . . . They are very supportive of your dreams and desires. They are a step in the right direction. And you've come to terms with Don (ex-husband). You don't hate him anymore.*

Woman: *I still have sadness and pain there where he's concerned.*

Man: *That will heal. It has healed a lot. You are and can be friendly now. That's part of letting go.*

Woman: *What do you think of Don?*

Man: *He competed with me and he abused your love, so I can't say I like him all that much. But you learned a lot about yourself and you let me get strong in your defense, so I think you and I got closer with each other.*

You see, I'm your brother . . . I protect and guide you sometimes. I support you. I complement you.

MALE AND FEMALE WITHIN

Male	Female
Intellect	Intuition
Reason	Emotion
Sun	Moon
Light	Dark
Shiva	Shakti
Work	Contemplation
People	Alone
Sex	Love
Eating	Cooking
Making money	Caring, nurturing
Leader	Responsive
Mental	Sensual
Destruction	Birth

CHAPTER SEVEN

Healing from the Inner Self

All healing comes from the Inner Self—the spiritual power that resides within each of us. This spiritual power has been given different names by many cultures and religions: God, Yahweh, Allah, Christ, Buddha, Shiva, Tao, the Great Goddess, Higher Power, Holy Spirit, Divine Mind, Higher Self, Cosmic Consciousness. I use the term Inner Self. Use whatever name is meaningful for you.

The Inner Self is the source of your true wisdom. It is like a radio transmitter, constantly sending out signals which must be picked up by an appropriate receiver in order to be understood. The Inner Self often "broadcasts" its guidance in the symbolic language of dreams, visual imagery, intuition, meditation, and other right-brain functions. Unless you pay attention, you can miss the profound truths that appear in these forms. For instance, dreams play an important role in maintaining the health of your psyche. However, your rational mind (left brain) doesn't understand dream language and dismisses it as irrelevant and unreal. Your intuition or inner knowing has suffered the same fate. You disparage intuition as being "only a hunch" and mistrust it on the grounds that it is not reasonable or logical.

This chapter provides simple techniques for decoding and understanding the wisdom of your Inner Healer as revealed in the symbolic language of dreams, visual imagery, and intuition. Through affirmations, meditation, and contemplation, you will learn the influence of the spiritual dimension upon the healing process.

DREAMS: REMEMBERING AND RECORDING

Here are some simple methods for remembering your dreams and for recording them (to be interpreted later on):

1. Keep the journal and pens within reach so that you can use them as soon as you wake up.

2. Before going to sleep, tell yourself:
   I will remember my dreams when I wake up. I will recall especially the dreams guiding me toward better health.

3. When you wake up, keep your eyes closed and review the major points in your dream(s). Go over each image and *fix it* in your mind. Recall any sounds or speech you heard, colors you saw, or other sensations or experiences.

Note: If you wish, tell your dream aloud into a tape recorder. Tell it in the first person, present tense, i.e., "I'm walking down a path. . . ."

4. Open your eyes. Draw the dream images in your journal. Then write the dream out, using the first person, present tense.

5. When you have time, interpret your dream(s), using the methods pre-presented in the following exercises.

Benefits: This is a method of training yourself to remember your dreams so that you will have the raw material from which to draw dream interpretation.

THE DREAM BODY

The drawing and dialoguing presented throughout this book have prepared you to decode your dreams. Hopefully, you have become accustomed to the language of imagery and symbols, and feel familiar with this form of communication.

One very simple means of interpreting a dream is as follows:

If you have a dream about your physical condition, draw a picture of the image(s) that appeared in the dream or write about any other perception you had. It may have been a body sensation or other sense impression. Perhaps some words were spoken that told you something about your physical condition.

If you drew a visual image, have a dialogue with it. Let each part of the picture speak. If an illness appeared in the dream, let the illness speak. Let it tell you why it is appearing at this time and what it has come to teach you. Ask your body what you can do to help it feel better. Write the questions with your dominant hand; let your body or the physical condition write through your non-dominant hand.

Benefits: This exercise can help you tune into the early warnings your dreams often contain. If you are alert to the messages in dreams, you will get much more in touch with the sources of illness and healing that live within you.

Note: When you have a dream in which you experience unusual or vivid bodily sensations (flying or falling), write a description of it in the present tense. If the experience was frightening, rewrite the dream with a happy ending. For instance, instead of falling and being hurt, allow yourself to be transformed into a bird, a butterfly, a balloon, or grow wings yourself. Create some imaginative solution to the problem. Remember, it's your dream and you can do whatever you want with it.

THE HEALING DREAM

If you are ill or in physical or emotional pain and want to initiate the healing process, ask your Inner Self for a healing dream. Make the request before falling asleep. It is important that you have faith in your Inner Self and that you relax into sleep, trusting that you have a source of healing power within which will respond to your sincere and faithful request for help.

You may want to write an actual letter to your Inner Self, asking for a healing dream. Date the letter and sign it as if you were writing to a friend. Thank your Inner Self for any loving guidance it may give you. For example:

December 13

Dear Inner Self,

If it is your will, please give me a dream tonight which will help guide me in the healing process for my chronic lower back pain. Thank you for everything you have given me and continue to give me.

Love, Valerie

Draw an image that appears in your healing dream. Let the image speak through your non-dominant hand, giving you any wisdom or practical information it has to offer at this time.

Describe in detail any physical sensations or emotional reactions you had in the dream.

Benefits: This is the way to recognize and activate your inner healing powers. If you approach these dreams with an open mind and a receptive, grateful heart, they will repay you with many blessings.

LEFT HAND DIALOGUE WITH LITTLE GIRL
AND THE COLLAR FROM A DREAM IMAGE:

My collar—remember my collar—a symbol of communication—creativity—beauty—the Goddess coming your way. Where is my playmate? I can grow to a Goddess with my playmate. I want my soul playmate and not worry about adult things. I want to live and laugh. I want to please and make happy. I do not want to be denied or bossed. I want what I want now and no waiting. I want to sing and dance. Let me draw—wear pretty clothes and pretty colors. I want to have my own way but live in harmony and not under dictatorship. I want to grow and play and be nourished by my Mother and my Father.

THE HEALER WITHIN

Do the *Breathing Meditation* and allow yourself to relax fully. Contemplate the "the Healer Within." Allow an image of the "Inner Healer" to form. What does this image look like? If you don't see a picture, then allow a feeling, a sensation, or a presence. (We "image" with all our senses, so don't restrict yourself.) Feel the quality of the Inner Healer's presence.

Let the Healer take you to a beautiful, safe environment. It may be one that you create in your imagination or it may be a memory of a place you've been before. Allow yourself to experience the environment fully: listen to the sounds, smell the odors, touch the things around you, and look at things carefully (colors, shapes, objects, textures, etc.). Let the loving energy from the Healer and the environment fill your whole being. Be receptive to the beauty and peace that is surrounding and penetrating you.

Draw a picture of your Healer and have a written dialogue with both hands. Let the Healer speak with your non-dominant hand, and *you* speak with your dominant hand.

Benefits: This is an extension of *The Healing Dream,* except that here you activate the Inner Healer *while in a conscious state.* This makes the Healer available to you whenever you wish.

DIALOGUE WITH THE INNER HEALER

Right Hand: Who are you?

Left Hand: *I am your Inner Healer. I coordinate the whole show.*

Right Hand: What's going on with my neck?

Left Hand: *You still aren't grounded. Too much nervous energy. It's hard for you to get through a day without stressing your weak spots. You're doing better, though. You must be pure of heart & brave. You have to slay your dragons. You can't continue to float. Time is running out. The time is now. Own your power. You have disowned it for a decade. Heal & be strong. It is your destiny.*

Right Hand: Tell me what I should do to achieve this. How can I become your partner & cooperate in a trust of the heart?

Left Hand: *You should allow your pure intellect and discrimination to fully flower. Live with joy and dispassion. Let the heart flower under the protection of the pure intellect. Go for it! You are not here to hide your light. Let it shine but protect yourself. Don't be vulnerable to the world. Be conscious and let the Divine Energy envelop, protect and sustain you. That is all. Oh, you must walk everyday. Exercise daily. Meditate daily. Breathe and relax daily. This is part of your work.*

This is where I want to be
among the petals on the sea,
Flowing over curls and foam
Like Thumbalina sailing home.

GETTING CLEAR

Do *Breathing Meditation* (Chapter Two).

With eyes closed, imagine entering a beautiful room. It is very simply furnished and everything is white—the walls and carpeting are white and so are the few furnishings. The room is glowing with sunlight and brightness. It produces a wonderful feeling of serenity within you. Picture the room in detail.

Now, imagine time passing and the room becoming dusty, dirty, and soiled. It becomes cluttered with objects and bric-a-brac to the point that you can hardly move in the room. Suddenly, someone brings you a "magic solvent" and cleaning supplies. You clean the environment from top to bottom and throw out all the extraneous items. You bring the room back to its original condition: simple, serene, spotless, and glowing white. You enjoy the feelings of accomplishment and the bright, peaceful atmosphere in the room.

Meditate on some ways in which you can get clear in your own life. What areas in your own personal environment need cleaning or clearing? What personal possessions are you hanging onto even though you no longer need or use them? What foods and beverages can you eliminate from your diet? What activities can you drop from your life? Write a plan of action for "getting clear," for doing "spring cleaning" in your life. Make a list of things you can get rid of (give away, sell, loan out, etc.) to lighten your load. List the worries, problems, and burdens you want to dispose of at this time. Make a schedule of weekly "clearing" activities in all areas of your life. Take it a bit at a time, but do it consistently.

Benefits: Elimination is an essential function of the body and in all areas of life. Collected clutter and dirt clog up the creative, life-force channels. This exercise can help you lighten your life through discarding and purifying (inner and outer).

HEALTH AFFIRMATIONS

Create positive statements (affirmations) about your health. Write them in your journal. If you do not feel well right now, do the affirmations anyway. Write them in the present tense. This can help you reprogram from a negative, sickness-oriented frame of mind to a positive, healthy one. It is important to create your own affirmations, ones that reflect your own expression of health. Here are a few ideas to inspire you:

"I'm feeling more energetic as time goes on."

"I am active and enjoying life more every day."

"I am taking good care of myself and my health improves daily."

"The more time and energy I spend in self-understanding and self-care, the better I feel."

"I enjoy excellent health and vitality."

Write one or more health affirmations each day. Meditate upon being healthy and upon what health means to you.

See your body and your future life experiences with this new vibration of health. Write down how your life will be in the future with your new, positive attitude. How will you feel physically and emotionally? How will you behave? How will you relate to others?

Benefits: Affirmations are an important tool for transforming negative, pessimistic attitudes and beliefs into positive ones. Negative thoughts hypnotize or brainwash you into expecting the worst. Through affirmations you can consciously reprogram your thoughts to positive ones and create a more fulfilled and satisfying life. You can engage in a personal program of zest for life and "youthing" rather than automatically buying the common lies about aging, deterioration, and loss of vitality.

HEALING MYSELF

Make a HEALING HISTORY CHART, as shown in the illustration. Record illnesses, accidents, etc., you've experienced along with their date or year. Fill in the circumstances surrounding those periods in your life (the context, what was going on in your life just before and after the events). Write in the names of people, places, things, and activities you associate with the healing process. What made you feel better? What or who helped you become well? What did you do to help heal yourself?

Read over your complete HEALING HISTORY CHART. What do you notice there? Do you see any patterns? Are there any connections between the context of your illness and the illness itself? Any relationships between the illness, the context, and the healing process? Write about any connections you see.

Benefits: This exercise helps you explore your own personal experiences with healing. By reflecting upon what you actually went through, and how you survived and regained your health (if you did), you can gain insight into your own style of healing. You might also come to understand the role that illness plays in your life—how it contributes to your personal growth and regeneration by providing an opportunity to recharge your physical/emotional/mental batteries.

HEALING HISTORY CHART

YEAR/DATE	ILLNESS/ACCIDENT, ETC.	HEALING (PEOPLE, PLACES, THINGS, ACTIVITIES)

SOLITUDE

In order to contact your Inner Self, or spiritual dimension, it is necessary to spend some time alone to get to know yourself. Block out some time for solitude. You might want to go to a place in nature where you can be alone in peace and quiet, or find some environment which provides privacy and is free from outer distractions. Quietly focus on your own Inner Self. Listen to your thoughts, feelings, wishes, desires. Reflect upon your life at this time.

Write and/or draw your reflections in your journal.

Benefits: In this exercise, you are encouraged to provide time in which to get to know yourself better. Of course, that is primarily what journal-keeping (as presented in this book) is all about. If you have been doing these exercises, this experience of solitude will be familiar and probably very enriching for you.

SOLITARY ROSE

The sweetness of solitude surrounds me
solitary rose—fully alone
in meditation of my life,
the pattern of my days
stretching out around me—quietly
without distraction.

I return to myself
meeting my alone-ness with shyness
as in seeing an old friend
again
after some time
and events
and other people
have filled our lives
saying:

Ah yes, I have known you in other lives and times
known you in fear and desolation
known you in tears and desperation
and now in blessed familiarity and peace.

I wander in my days
as a tender fern growing toward the light
soaking up gentle showers of love
letting life in
letting myself happen
in my way
wandering through my garden
free to grow where I will.

LONELINESS AND LOVE

April 3

What is loneliness? What is love?

Loneliness. Feeling one's aloneness, separation, isolation, singleness. When I'm lonely, I often feel a longing for something. But what? Sometimes the empty space inside me wants to be filled—with work, with people, with words, with diversions.

At those times I often try to escape the emptiness, the no-thingness. Nothingness. Oblivion. Non-existence. That's what I'm afraid of. The feeling that I don't exist. That without another person to reflect me back to myself, I don't exist. But what about *me* reflecting me back to myself?

Loneliness feels like looking in the mirror and seeing no reflection. Isn't that what ghosts see—nothing—in the mirror? Loneliness is a lot like death, then. If no one is there, if no one mirrors me back to me, if no one answers me—then I am dead.

Loneliness also has an element of self-hatred and being forsaken, abandoned. Those early childhood fears of being deserted and left alone to die. Pretty basic stuff. . . .

Loneliness. I've struggled with it all my life. . . . But I always come back to myself. No matter what. . . .I only know that in the depths of my loneliness, in the darkest and deepest pits of myself, is my strength born. Not in any victories or praise or performance or applause. No, not in any of those places. Those are the by-products. No—the strength is in the bowels of fear, the terror of the night, the darkness of the soul. It is in that blackest night that the light penetrates me like a ray of sunlight. Without darkness, light has no meaning. . . .

I need my loneliness, for it is there that I fully embrace myself in pure simplicity.

MEDITATION

Find a quiet, private place which is comfortable and free from distractions and interruptions. Sit with your back erect and spine straight. Close your eyes and relax. (Use whatever relaxation technique you prefer.) Imagine your body being filled with white light, and surround yourself with a protective white light. See this light emanating from your body to about a foot all around.

Meditate for a few minutes upon your Inner Self, the spirit of God Within which gives you life. Ask your Inner Guide to help you in everyday life to move closer to your Divine Self and express it more fully.

Write about any significant images, symbols, intuitions, or thoughts that came to you while meditating.

Note: If you do not already meditate, begin with a few minutes each day and gradually increase it to fifteen minutes per sitting.

Benefits: This exercise is a simple means for beginning meditation. If you are already meditating, you are encouraged to continue. Meditation is an excellent way to develop your powers of intuition, creativity, spiritual insight, and self-healing.

PRAYER

Create an original prayer. Let it express your relationship with your Higher Power or Inner Self at this time in your life. Write your prayer out in your journal.

Benefits: Prayer has been used throughout the ages as mankind's bridge to the Spirit. It is a way of contacting the Divine dimension within ourselves, the Universal Mind, which is our true essence. Prayer has been used for supplication and invocation in time of need, and as a form of thanksgiving and joyful celebration of life. By creating your own personal prayer you can participate in this ancient form of human expression.

I'm letting God take care of me.

I'm letting God take me by the hand and lead the way.

All I ask is that I be helped to listen to God.

To hear my Higher Power, my Inner Self.

ENDINGS AND NEW BEGINNINGS

Reflect upon your beliefs and attitudes about death. What do you believe about death at this time in your life? How do your beliefs about death affect your everyday life? What is the significance of life to you? How does this belief affect you in practical terms: life goals, work, relationships, etc.?

Write your reflections upon life and death in your journal. What would you do if you knew you only had a year to live? A month? A week? A day?

Write about the death of a significant person in your life. How did that person's death affect you? What was the insight gained or the lesson learned?

If you've ever come close to death, write about the experience. What did you learn from it?

Benefits: This exercise is designed to lead you into an exploration of the ultimate questions of life and death. Such explorations can help you clarify your basic values, goals, and methods of achieving your aims in life. Alignment with your basic values and beliefs gives you a greater chance of achieving harmony within and without. When you lose contact with your higher purpose, then illness and confusion are apt to result.

FROM HERE TO THERE

My brother was 40 years old and I was standing by his bedside as he was dying. We were holding hands. He was very frightened.

It all happened over a year ago and, when I now think back to the "event" of his death, I realize I was frightened too. No one ever tells us anything about death, and why should they? Most of us don't want to hear about it anyway.

But there we were, at 9 o'clock on a dark snowy morning, surrounded by the sounds of normal hospital activity. Holding hands.

He asked me to help him and I knew he needed none of the physical assistance he had been requiring to sustain his life. Somehow I knew he was finishing his journey and was asking me to be his traveling companion for the next few steps. I agreed.

He said words and I listened. I said words and he listened. It's not even important what the words were, because when the words stopped . . . the true beauty began.

I have tried many times to explain what I saw in his face when he reached "the Light" and I always fall fathoms short. His eyes were brighter than a hundred children running to the tree on Christmas morning. His face was wisdom. He smiled as one does when seeing something very, very fine—or when a hard job has been completed, and it was well done. He was so, so happy.

He didn't need to hold my hand anymore. He was so involved with his world, his life in "the Light" that he was smiling, shaking hands invisible to me, and patting himself on the back. He told me who was there—Nana, Daddy, Uncle Bud, and more. He told me "they" were preparing a party for him because he "made it." He was so happy.

Looking directly at me, for the first time, he said, "It's so beautiful."

And that was that.

What a gift! What a gift my brother gave me. A gift of joy; a gift of comfort; a gift to share with as many people as will read or listen.

I am truly blessed. Thank you, Tom.

On Finding a Health Professional

There are many methods for finding a health professional. Everyone is different and needs to find the way that is right for him or her. I have found that the reasons for finding a healer may differ from one person to the next, or they may change within one's lifetime. Some are motivated by a serious illness, as I was. The pain and disease had become so severe, I simply HAD to get help. Others seek out a health guide because they want to maintain optimal health, thereby preventing illness. That is the philosophical premise of Chinese Medicine (acupuncture, acupressure, T'ai Chi Ch'uan, herbal remedies): *stay balanced and stay well.*

As for finding a healer or health guide, let me suggest some approaches that have worked for my clients, students, and me.

1. *Ask yourself, "What do I want?"*

It's important to know what kind of health care you want. What kind of personality, manner, training, and approaches do you want in a health professional? Some people only trust a person who has M.D. after their name. If that's your preference, find out *what kind of M.D.* you want. Or you might ask, "What kind *don't* I want?" Some physicians and health care professionals can be insensitive and intimidating and display a patronizing know-it-all manner. One of my friends calls these types "M. Deities" because of their tendency to "play God." If you have had bad experiences with medical care, write down what the negative characteristics of the person or the situation were. Then write down *how you want it to be.*

When I was pregnant with my first child, the Obstetrician/Gynecologist came into the examining room smoking a cigar! I didn't want that smoke and smell around me or my baby, so I insisted that his partner in the medical practice be the one to deliver my baby. And I got what I wanted.

During my second pregnancy, I became interested in natural childbirth, so I selected an Ob/Gyn who used hypnosis and a modified Lamaze Method. During the delivery I was fully awake and watched my daughter being born. It was wonderful! It took me two births and four Ob/Gyn's but I finally got things the way I wanted them. Getting clearer and clearer about what kind of health care you want will enable you to have it your way. If you aren't satisfied with the kind of professional health care you are getting, then visualize how you'd like it to be. Picture it in your mind. This will make it a reality. Draw a picture of it. Make two lists in your journal:

WHAT I WANT.   WHAT I DON'T WANT

If you're exploring methods of healing or health maintenance other than the ones you have been using, ask yourself: What do I want and how do I want to feel? Describe it in your journal. For me, this happened in a dream in which I was being treated by a truly healing person. I awoke feeling much better. It was such a powerful image that it allowed me to see the possibilities of being with a healer I trusted. Right afterward, I found a healer just like the one in the dream.

2. Ask a friend

If you have a particular health problem, be alert to the experiences of those who have had the same problem and handled it effectively. During my illness a close friend whom I trusted first recommended holistic health care (mentioned in Chapter One). When she referred me to her own practitioner, I followed my friend's advice because I had confidence in her. We had similar values and I also felt that she genuinely cared about my well-being. After what I had been through, she understood that I didn't want to go to someone who was insensitive, too busy to spend time with me, or too overworked to offer me quality health care.

Asking friends for referrals to health practitioners can also work when you are *not* ill, but simply want to improve your health. Noticing a dramatic change in my friend Jane's posture and energy level over a few weeks, I asked her what she was doing. Dieting? Exercising? It was Rolfing, she replied, and explained that Rolfing was a program of deep tissue massage that releases stress and build-up of physical/emotional/mental tensions.

"That's for me," I said, and enrolled in a series of Rolfing sessions. I wasn't looking for a remedy to an illness, I just wanted better posture and more energy. And I got it.

3. *Attend demonstrations and seminars.*

If you want to know more about healing and health, I suggest you attend some lectures or demonstrations. You'll have to research what is available in your geographical location. Many cities have health directories and local publications which feature health services and self-help programs.

4. *Go for a one-time trial session.*

Most professionals encourage potential clients to come in for one paid consultation as an assessment. This gives both the client and the professional an opportunity to see if they work together. Furthermore, the client can explain his/her reasons for seeking help, ask questions about the treatment being offered, and inquire about the fees. Personal health goals can be discussed in light of the methods being used by the professional. Such a session also enables the client to experience the professional's personality and environment, two key elements in health care.

5. *Read books and periodicals.*

There are thousands of books for the layperson on all aspects of health and healing. Some of them are listed in the Bibliography and are grouped according to subject matter or themes. There are many more health books in libraries, bookstores, and shops specializing in self-help books. I suggest you go to one of these sources and browse around. Let your intuition lead you to the books that are appropriate for you at this time. You'll know when you've found a "friend" among all the books available on the subject.

QUALITIES TO LOOK FOR IN A HEALTH PROFESSIONAL

1. *Practices what he/she preaches.*

The individual is a living example of the methods and approaches being used in the professional practice. For instance, my T'ai Chi Ch'uan teacher is a calm, relaxed, physically healthy individual. I learn as much about how to be healthy from simply being around her as I do from the formal instruction.

2. *Loves the work he/she is doing.*

The individual believes in the methods being used, is enthusiastic about them, and applies them in everyday life. The practitioner also loves working with people and has faith in the self-healing ability of the client. The practitioner's positive attitude about the work and the client is a key.

3. *Has depth of knowledge/training and breadth of experience.*

Formal study combined with personal experience is the best combination in professional preparation. The blending of theory (understanding) with practice yields wisdom. These are the signs of a fine health practitioner. A well-developed intuition is also extremely important, so that the practitioner can sense what your particular needs are, and how best to meet them. Also, look for a personality that harmonizes with your own. In the medical profession this has been called a "good bedside manner." This is very personal and individual, like your taste in food, music, or colors. Listen to your own feelings and hunches. After all, it's *your* healing and *your* health.

BIBLIOGRAPHY

BODY/MIND

Borysenko, Joan. *Minding the Body, Mending the Mind.* New York: Bantam Books, 1988.

Cousins, Norman. *Anatomy of an Illness.* New York: W. W. Norton, 1979.

————. *The Healing Heart,* New York: Avon Books, 1983.

Dychtwald, Ken. *Bodymind.* New York: Jove Publications, Inc., 1978.

Hay, Louise. *You Can Heal Your Life.* Santa Monica, CA: Hay House, 1987.

Joy, Brugh. *Joy's Way.* Los Angeles: J. P. Tarcher, 1978.

Kurtz, Ron and Hector Prestera. *The Body Reveals.* New York: Harper and Row, 1976.

Mindell, Arnold. *Working with the Dreaming Body.* Boston: Routledge & Paul, 1985.

Pelletier, Kenneth R. *Mind as Healer, Mind as Slayer.* New York: Dell, 1977.

Sanford, John A. *Healing and Wholeness.* New York: Paulist Press, 1977.

Selye, Hans, M.D. *The Stress of Life.* New York: McGraw Hill, 1978.

Strozzi-Heckler, Richard. *Anatomy of Change: Awakening the Wisdom of the Body.* Boston: Shambhala, 1984.

SELF-HELP AND SELF-CARE

Ardell, Donald B. *High Level Wellness.* Emmaus, PA: Rodale Press, 1977.

Bates, W. H. *Better Eyesight Without Glasses.* New York: Pyramid, 1971.

Benson, Herbert. *The Relaxation Response.* New York: Avon Books, 1976.

Berkus, Rusty. *To Heal Again: Toward Serenity and the Resolution of Grief.* Encino, CA: Red Rose Press, 1984.

Chang, Stephen. The Complete System of Self-Healing: Internal Exercises. San Francisco: Tao Press, 1986.

Chia, Mantak. *Taoist Ways to Transform Stress Into Vitality.* Huntington, NY: Healing Tao Books, 1985.

Chopra, Deepak. *Creating Health: Beyond Prevention, Toward Perfection.* Boston: Houghton Mifflin, 1987.

De Smedt, Evelyn, et al. *Lifearts: A Practical Guide to Total Being—New Medicine and Ancient Wisdom.* New York: St. Martin's, 1977.

Gilmore, Timothy, et al. *About the Tomatis Method.* Toronto: The Listening Centre Press, 1988. (Communication and learning system based on listening.)

Hay, Louise. *I Love My Body.* Santa Monica, CA: Hay House, 1987.

Jaffe, Dennis T. *Healing From Within.* New York: Alfred A. Knopf, 1980.

Kapit, Winn and Lawrence Elson. *The Anatomy Coloring Book.* New York: Harper and Row, 1977.

Kushi, Michio. *An Introduction to Oriental Diagnosis.* London: Red Moon Press, 1976.

Lad, Vasant. *Ayurveda: The Science of Self-Healing.* Santa Fe, NM: Lotus Press, 1984.

Locke, Stephen and Douglas Colligan. *The Healer Within.* New York: Dutton: 1986.

Muramoto, Naboru. *Healing Ourselves.* New York: Avon Books, 1973.

Ryan, Regina Sara and John W. Travis, M.D. *Wellness Workbook.* Berkeley, CA: Ten Speed Press, 1981.

Samuels, Mike, M.D., and Hal Bennet. *Be Well.* New York: Random House/Bookworks, 1975.

Satir, Virginia. *Self-Esteem.* Berkeley, Celestial Arts, 1975.

Shutz, Will and Evelyne Turner. *Body Fantasy.* San Francisco: Harper and Row, 1976.

Segal, Jeanne. *Feeling Great.* North Hollywood, CA: Newcastle Publishing, 1987.

Simonton, O. Carl, M.D., Stephanie Mathews-Simonton, and James L. Creighton. *Getting Well Again.* New York: Bantam Books, 1978.

Stone Randolph. *Health Building: The Conscious Art of Living Well.* Reno, NV: CRCS Publications, 1985.

Ullman, Dana and Stephen Cummings. *Everybody's Guide to Homeopathic Medicines: Taking Care of Yourself and Your Family with Safe and Effective Remedies.* Los Angeles: Jeremy Tarcher, 1984.

HEALING, MASSAGE, AND BODYWORK

Brennan, Barbara Ann. *Hands of Light: A Guide to Healing Through the Human Energy Field.* New York: Bantam Books, 1987.

Gordon, Richard. *Your Healing Hands.* Santa Cruz, CA: Unity Press, 1978.

Gunther, Bernard. *Energy Ecstasy.* North Hollywood, CA: Newcastle Publishing, 1983.

Heller, Joseph and William Henkin. *Bodywise: Regaining Your Natural Flexibility and Vitality for Maximum Well-Being.* Los Angeles: Jeremy Tarcher, 1986.

Krieger, Dolores. *The Therapeutic Touch: How to Use Your Hands to Help or to Heal.* New York: Prentice-Hall, 1979.

Lidell, Lucinda. *The Book of Massage.* New York: Simon & Schuster, 1984.

Miller, Roberta De Long. *Psychic Massage.* New York: Harper & Row, 1975.

Rolf, Ida. *Rolfing—The Integration of Human Structures.* New York: Harper & Row, 1977.

Seidman, Maruti. *A Guide to Polarity Therapy.* North Hollywood, CA: Newcastle Publishing, 1982.

Teeguarden, Iona. *The Joy of Feeling: Bodymind Acupressure.* Tokyo & Boston: Japan Publications, 1987.

DIET, NUTRITION, AND WEIGHT CONTROL

Arenson, Gloria. *How to Stop Playing the Weighting Game.* Los Angeles: Transformation Publications, 1978.

Capacchione, Lucia and Elizabeth Johnson. *Lighten Up Journal: Making Friends with Your Body.* Santa Monica, CA: InnerWorks, 1988.

Colbin, Annemarie. *Food and Healing.* New York: Ballantine Books, 1986.

_____. *The Book of Whole Meals.* New York: Ballantine Books, 1983.

Diamond, Harvey and Marilyn. *Fit For Life.* New York: Warner Books, 1985.

Orbach, Susie. *Fat Is a Feminist Issue.* New York: Paddington, 1978.

Pritikin, Nathan. *The Pritikin Program for Diet and Exercise*. New York: Bantam Books, 1980.

Robbins, John. *Diet for a New America: How Your Food Choices Affect Your Health, Happiness, and the Future of Life on Earth*. Walpole, NH, Stillpoint, 1987.

Robertson, Laurel. *The New Laurel's Kitchen*. Berkeley, CA: Ten Speed Press, 1986.

Roth, Geneen. *Feeding the Hungry Heart: The Experience of Compulsive Eating*. New York: The Bobbs-Merrill Company, 1984.

MOVEMENT AND EXERCISE

Feldenkrais, Moshe. *Awareness Through Movement*. New York: Harper & Row, 1972.

Hittleman, Richard. *Richard Hittleman's Yoga 28-Day Exercise Plan*. New York: Workman Publishing Co., 1975.

Huang, Wen-Shan. *Fundamentals of Tai Chi Ch'uan*. Seattle, WA: South Sky Book Co., 1982.

Iyengar, B.K.S. *Light on Yoga* (Revised Edition). New York: Schocken Books, 1979.

Smith, David. *The East/West Exercise Book*. New York: McGraw Hill, 1976.

VISUALIZATION, IMAGERY, AND AFFIRMATION

Achterberg, Jean. *Imagery and Healing: Shamanism and Modern Medicine*. Boston: Shambhala, 1985.

Assagioli, Robert. *Psychosynthesis*. New York: Viking, 1971.

Gawain, Shakti. *Creative Visualization*. New York: Bantam Books, 1979.

———. *Living in the Light*. Berkeley, CA: Whatever Publishing, 1986.

Gendlin, Eugene. *Focusing*. New York: Bantam Books, 1982.

Hay, Louise. *Heal Your Body* (Revised Edition). Santa Monica, CA: Hay House, 1982.

Jampolsky, Gerald. *There Is a Rainbow Behind Every Dark Cloud*. Berkeley, CA: Celestial Arts, 1978.

Long, Max Freedom. *The Secret Science Behind Miracles.* Marina del Rey, CA: DeVorss, 1954.

Rossman, Martin L., M.D. *Healing Yourself: A Step-by-Step Program for Better Health through Imagery.* New York: Walker and Co., 1987.

Samuels, Mike, M.D., and Nancy Samuels. *Seeing with the Mind's Eye.* New York and Berkeley, CA: Random House, 1975.

Sheikh, Anees, ed. *Imagination and Healing.* Amityville, NY: Baywood, 1984.

Shorr, Joseph E., Dr. *Go See the Movie in Your Head.* New York: Popular Library, 1977.

PSYCHOTHERAPY AND SELF-THERAPY

Capacchione, Lucia. *The Creative Journal: The Art of Finding Yourself.* Chicago: Ohio University/Swallow Press, 1979.

Moustakas, Clark E. *Loneliness and Love.* New Jersey: Prentice-Hall, 1972.

Stone, Christopher. *Re-Creating Your Self.* Portland, OR: Metamorphous, 1988.

Stone, Hal and Sidra Winkelman. *Embracing Our Selves* (Revised Edition). Berkeley, CA: New World Library, 1989.

VIBRATIONAL HEALING: SOUND, COLOR, GEMS, AND PLANTS

Babbitt, Edwin. *Principles of Light and Color.* Secaucus, NJ: Lyle Stuart, 1980.

Clark, Linda. *The Ancient Art of Color Therapy.* New York: Pocket Books, 1975.

Chase, Pamela and Jonathan Pawlik. *The Newcastle Guide to Healing with Crystals.* North Hollywood, CA: Newcastle Publishing, 1988.

————. *The Newcastle Guide to Healing with Gemstones.* North Hollywood, CA: Newcastle Publishing, 1989.

David, William. *The Harmonics of Sound, Color and Vibration: A System for Self-Awareness and Soul Evolution.* Marina del Rey, CA: DeVorss, 1980.

Gerber, Richard, M.D. *Vibrational Medicine: New Choices for Healing Ourselves.* Santa Fe, NM: Bear and Company, 1988.

Khan, Hazrat Inayat. *The Music of Life.* New Lebanon, NY: Omega Press, 1983.

Keyes. Laurel. *Toning: The Creative Power of the Voice.* Marina del Rey, CA: DeVorss, 1973.

Lad, Vasant and David Frawley. *The Yoga of Herbs: An Ayurvedic Guide to Herbal Medicine.* Santa Fe, Lotus Press, 1986.

Ouseley, S. G. J. *The Power of the Rays: The Science of Color Healing.* Essex, England: L. N. Fowler & Co., 1951.

Raphaell, Katrina. *Crystal Healing.* New York: Aurora Press, 1987.

Vithoulhas, George. *Homeopathy: Medicine of the New Man.* New York: Arco, 1979.

CREATIVITY AND SELF-DISCOVERY

Brookes, Mona. *Drawing with Children.* Los Angeles: Jeremy P. Tarcher, 1986.

Capacchione, Lucia. *The Power of Your Other Hand.* North Hollywood, CA: Newcastle Publishing, 1988.

_____. *The Creative Journal: The Art of Finding Yourself.* Athens, OH: Ohio University/Swallow Press, 1979.

_____. *The Creative Journal for Children.* Santa Monica, CA: Inner-Works, 1988.

_____. *The Creative Journal for Teens.* Santa Monica, CA: InnerWorks, 1988.

Edwards, Betty. *Drawing on the Right Side of the Brain.* Los Angeles: Jeremy P. Tarcher, 1979.

Jung, C. G. *Man and His Symbols.* New York: Doubleday, 1964.

_____. *Mandala Symbolism.* Princeton, NJ: Princeton University Press, 1972.

Vaughn, Frances. *Awakening Intuition.* New York: Doubleday, 1979.

MALE AND FEMALE

Bolen, Jean Shinoda, M.D. *Goddesses in Everywoman.* San Francisco: Harper & Row, 1984.

Harding, Esther M. *Woman's Mysteries*. New York: Bantam Books, 1973.

Johnson, Robert. *He*. New York: Harper & Row, 1977.

_____. *She*. New York: Harper & Row, 1977.

_____. *We*. San Francisco: Harper & Row, 1983.

Jung, Emma. *Animus and Anima*. Zurich, Switzerland: Spring Publishing, 1978.

Leonard, Linda. *The Wounded Woman*. Boston: Shambhala, 1986.

_____. *On the Way to the Wedding: Transforming the Love Relationship*. Boston: Shambhala, 1986.

Sanford, John A. *The Invisible Partners*. New York: Paulist Press, 1980.

DREAMS

Capacchione, Lucia. *The Creative Journal: The Art of Finding Yourself* (Chapter 6: "What Your Higher Self Knows"). Athens, OH: Ohio University/Swallow Press, 1988.

Faraday, Anne. *Dream Power*. New York: Berkeley, 1973.

Garfield, Patricia. *Creative Dreaming*. New York: Ballantine Books, 1974.

Johnson, Robert. *Inner Work: Using Dreams and Active Imagination for Personal Growth*. New York: Harper & Row, 1987.

La Berge, Stephen. *Lucid Dreaming: The Power of Being Aware in Your Dreams*. New York: Ballantine, 1986.

INNER SELF AND SPIRITUAL AWARENESS

Bach, Richard. *Illusions*. New York: Delacorte Press, 1977.

Fields, Rick. *Chop Wood, Carry Water: A Guide to Finding Spiritual Fulfillment in Everyday Life*. Los Angeles: Jeremy P. Tarcher, 1984.

Goldstein, Joseph. *The Experience of Insight: A Simple and Direct Guide to Buddhist Meditation*. Boston: Shambhala, 1983.

Hayes, Peter. *The Supreme Adventure*. New York: Dell Publishing, 1988.

Jampolsky, Gerald. M.D. *Love Is Letting Go of Fear*. Millbrae, CA: Celestial Arts, 1979.

_____. *Teach Only Love: The Seven Principles of Attitudinal Healing*. New York: Bantam Books, 1983.

Le Shan, Lawrence. *How to Meditate: A Guide to Self-Discovery*. New York: Bantam Books, 1974.

Levine, Steven. *A Gradual Awakening*. New York: Doubleday, 1979.

Muktananda, Swami. *I Am That*. South Fallsburg, NY: SYDA Foundation, 1978.

_____. Meditate. South Fallsburg, NY: SYDA Foundation, 1980.

_____. *Where Are You Going?* South Fallsburg, NY: SYDA Foundation, 1981.

_____. *Reflections of the Self*. South Fallsburg, NY: SYDA Foundation, 1980.

Suzuki, Shunryu. *Zen Mind, Beginner's Mind*. New York: Weatherhill, 1970.

Tulku, Tarthang. *Gesture of Balance: A Guide to Self-Healing, Awareness, and Meditation*. Berkeley, CA: Dharma Press, 1976.

LIFE-THREATENING ILLNESSES

AIDS Project Los Angeles. *AIDS: A Self-Care Manual*. Los Angeles: IBS Press, 1987.

Badgley, Laurence. *Healing AIDS Naturally*. New York: Human Energy Press, 1987.

Benjamin, Harold. *From Victim to Victor: The Story of the Wellness Community*. Los Angeles: Jeremy P. Tarcher, 1988.

Hay, Louise L. *The AIDS Book: Creating a Positive Approach*. Santa Monica, CA: Hay House, 1988.

Moffatt, B. C. *When Someone You Love Has AIDS*. Santa Monica, CA: IBS Press, 1986.

Segal, Jeanne. *Living Beyond Fear: A Course for Coping with the Emotional Aspects of Life-Threatening Illnesses*. North Hollywood, CA: Newcastle Publishing, 1984.

Serinus, Jason, ed. *Psychoimmunity and the Healing Process: A Holistic Approach to Immunity and AIDS*. Berkeley, CA: Celestial Arts, 1987.

Siegel, Bernard, M.D. *Love, Medicine, and Miracles*. New York: Harper & Row, 1986.

DEATH AND DYING

Johnson, Elizabeth. *As Someone Dies*. Santa Monica, Hay House, 1988.

Kubler-Ross, Elisabeth, M.D. *On Death and Dying*, New York: Collier, 1970.

Levine, Stephen. *Who Dies? An Investigation of Conscious Living and Conscious Dying.* New York: Doubleday, 1982.

———. *Meetings at the Edge: Dialogues with the Grieving and the Dying, the Healing and the Healed.* New York: Doubleday. 1984.

Moody, Raymond. *Life After Life.* New York, Bantam Books, 1986.

ORACLES FOR INNER GUIDANCE

Blum, Ralph. *The Book of Runes.* New York: St. Martin's Press, 1982.

Connolly, Eileen. *Tarot: A New Handbook for the Apprentice.* North Hollywood, CA: Newcastle Publishing, 1979.

Greer, Mary. *Tarot for Your Self: A Workbook for Personal Transformation.* North Hollywood, CA: Newcastle Publishing, 1984.

Wilhelm, Richard and Cary Baynes. *The I Ching or Book of Changes.* Princeton, NJ: Bollingen, 1950.

Wing, R. L. *The I Ching Workbook,* New York: Doubleday, 1979.